Not Far
Tree *From the*

Kent W. Henderson

Not Far From the Tree

TATE PUBLISHING
AND ENTERPRISES, LLC

Not Far From the Tree
Copyright © 2014 by Kent W. Henderson. All rights reserved.

No part of this publication may be reproduced, stored in a retrieval system or transmitted in any way by any means, electronic, mechanical, photocopy, recording or otherwise without the prior permission of the author except as provided by USA copyright law.

This novel is a work of fiction. Names, descriptions, entities, and incidents included in the story are products of the author's imagination. Any resemblance to actual persons, events, and entities is entirely coincidental.

The opinions expressed by the author are not necessarily those of Tate Publishing, LLC.

Published by Tate Publishing & Enterprises, LLC
127 E. Trade Center Terrace | Mustang, Oklahoma 73064 USA
1.888.361.9473 | www.tatepublishing.com

Tate Publishing is committed to excellence in the publishing industry. The company reflects the philosophy established by the founders, based on Psalm 68:11,
"*The Lord gave the word and great was the company of those who published it.*"

Book design copyright © 2014 by Tate Publishing, LLC. All rights reserved.
Cover design by Rtor Maghuyop
Interior design by Jake Muelle

Published in the United States of America
ISBN: 978-1-62902-927-6
1. Fiction / Historical
2. Fiction / Family Life
14.01.03

Dedication

To my beloved wife, Roma

Table of Contents

Preface 9

Hardship and Self-Pity. 11

Brooms and Tanning Lotion. 22

Laughter and Tears. 30

Hating Chickens. 73

Sheep, Turkeys, and Tutors 81

Welcome to Logo. 90

Working on the Railroad 115

Bonding 133

Sweat and Debt 164

The War. 182

The Bride 198

Revelation. 209

Better Days. 223

Preface

The past few days haven't been much fun for twelve-year-old Carl Spader. He is overwhelmed with homework even though the school year will soon end. His best friend, Abraham, is going on vacation, and Carl will be staying home—as usual. The Spader family is poor with seemingly no prospect for a better future.

Carl's internal conflicts fester. One evening when he is no longer able to contain his emotions, he suddenly and angrily cries out to his parents, "Am I adopted? Don't I have grandparents? Why don't we ever talk about them? Is Mike my brother, or did we both come from some orphanage? Why can't we go on vacations, and why don't we have any money?"

The outburst catches his parents by surprise, but they don't get angry, nor do they chastise him for asking.

For several hours, Bill and Ruth patiently tell their sons about their own lives and those of their previous generations. Carl and his brother Mike listen spellbound as they learn about their ancestors. By the time his parents are through talking, Carl's opinion of his family will be changed forever.

Hardship and Self-Pity

Something was definitely wrong, and young Carl Spader wasn't himself. He was silent as he walked along the asphalt pavement next to his brother, Michael.

On any normal day after the brothers left school, they would cheerfully walk or run the nine blocks to their home, laughing and playing games. Usually they would visit with each other while passing the time kicking rocks, cans, or sticks that littered the side of the of the highway, but this particular Friday was different. Carl was obviously in a depressed mood. He didn't want to talk with his brother, and if Mike kicked a rock or can in Carl's direction, Carl would just give Mike an irritated look and step over the object rather than kick it. Mike eventually quit trying to play or make conversation. They trudged toward their hillside home in spiritless silence. It was a typically beautiful San Diego day. The sun was shining, and there was a cool ocean breeze weaving its way through the ocean-side buildings, searching for the nearby mountains. After dodging their way between cars and trucks to cross the highway, they trudged their way up the steep hill toward their home.

Perspiring after the long hot walk, the brothers entered their house, and after shouting friendly greetings to their mother, both of them collapsed into one of the four high-back wooden chairs positioned around the small kitchen table. Since it was after four o'clock, they knew that their father had already left for work to perform his evening custodial job.

"Would you boys like to go with me while I pick up some groceries?" Carl's mother asked.

Mike quickly jumped to his feet, almost knocking over the chair, eager to get away from his irritable brother for a while.

"Carl, do you also want to come along?" Ruth asked.

Carl shook his head very slowly without answering or making eye contact with his mother. "You two have a splendid time!" Carl sarcastically responded, his eyes never leaving the table.

Mike was two years younger than Carl, but at age ten, he was almost as tall as his brother. Usually they were exceptionally close, but this particular Friday afternoon, Carl definitely wanted to be home and alone and not wandering around the aisles in some crowded grocery store. Besides, whenever his mother went shopping, she always seemed to find a neighbor or friend who wanted to endlessly chatter about insignificant things. Carl was relieved to simply remain home.

Ruth seemed to understand Carl's mood and replied pleasantly. "We should be back within a couple of hours. There is fresh bread in the bread box if you are hungry, but don't eat so much that you will spoil your appetite for supper," she said.

Most people have down days, and today it was Carl's turn to feel depressed and full of self-pity. He couldn't exactly put his finger on any specific event that prompted his feelings; it seemed to be a culmination of many things, but the tough homework assignment probably was the final straw.

With only one school day left in the year, why had his teacher, Ms. Brinkley, given him such a hopelessly difficult weekend assignment? It wasn't just one assignment but three. The first was to write a story about his favorite friend and explain what characteristics that friend possessed that made him so special. The second was to write about his favorite family vacation, and the third was to write a short history about his parents and grandparents. Each assignment was to be two pages or longer, and the reports were due on Monday.

Carl had recently turned twelve years old and was in the sixth grade. It didn't seem reasonable to stack that much homework on any person the last official day of school. It just plain wasn't fair! Carl thought about postponing writing the assignments until Sunday, but he knew his mother would never stand for procrastination.

He might as well get started while he had some quiet time.

He cut a slice of homemade bread, and after spreading it with margarine, he sprinkled on some brown sugar and a pinch of cinnamon before heading to the bedroom he shared with his brother. The room wasn't large, but then again, neither was the house. He sat down at the small wooden antique table and laid a piece of lined paper in front of him. He stared at the paper for several minutes before he wrote a single word.

Carl was grateful that the first assignment had to do with writing about a friend. Other than Mike, his best friend was Abraham Stein. Abe was the son of a prominent and renowned San Diego dental surgeon. It would be easy for Carl to write about Abe because he was such a great guy. Carl leaned back in the armless chair and thought back to when he and Abe first met. Carl then started making a list of all of the characteristics he liked about his friend. Carl numbered each of the positive attributes in the order of what he considered to be the most important. As he thought about his assignment, he leaned back in his chair and gazed at the cracks in the ceiling. He let his mind wander back to when he and his family first moved into their hillside home.

His father, William "Bill" Spader, had served in the army during the Second World War and had been severely wounded in combat. Carl didn't know much about his father's military service or about his injuries, other than whatever the injury had been, it now prevented him from doing strenuous work that required heavy lifting or extended standing.

After Bill was discharged from the army in 1945, he and Ruth moved to Pocatello, Idaho. In January, 1947, Bill's health worsened, probably aggravated by the cold winters, and it became necessary for he and Ruth to relocate to a warmer climate near a veteran's hospital.

Carl met Abraham Stein on the first day of school. Both boys were in the third grade and were alphabetically seated next to one another. They immediately became good friends, and at school they ate lunch together, studied, and played sports. In their free time they went to the beach or hiked. Their friendship had continued for four wonderful years, but that would all change when school commenced again in the fall, and that thought did nothing to improve Carl's attitude.

The friends would both be entering junior high school in three months, but unfortunately, they would be enrolled in different schools. Abe would be going to a newly constructed private school located closer to his home. Carl would be going to a run-down older school that had a bad reputation. Carl wasn't looking forward to the new school year.

Thankfully, the boys would have three glorious months to sun themselves on the beaches, hike the hills, play baseball, and do things that are truly important, none of which would have anything to do with school. Abe was an only child, and he and Carl were as close as most brothers.

Whether their friendship would continue after the summer ended, only time would tell.

Carl was large for his age, and with his sandy hair and brown eyes, he favored his father. Abe had a similar build but was four inches shorter than Carl and was agile, fleet of foot, and was an exceptionally bright student. Whenever an important decision had to be made, it was generally Abe who found an alternative.

Carl's home was located near the school division boundary, one mile from the elementary school. Abe and Carl lived three miles apart but happened to be in the same school district. To be eligible to ride the school bus, a student had to live ten or more blocks from the school. Carl and Mike were the only two students in the district living east of the school who didn't qualify to ride. Carl's mother had pleaded her son's cases, but her appeals always fell on uncompassionate ears. Rules were rules, and no one wanted to rock the boat. Abe caught the school bus right in front of his house, and it took him to the school parking lot.

Abe's father was a renowned dental surgeon, and his home and late-model automobiles were symbols of his success. Carl's father was a custodian—a lowly janitor. He worked his low-paying job at night, cleaning windows, scrubbing floors, and sanitizing toilets.

Many times Abe invited Carl to play at his home, and Carl seldom refused. Carl never invited Abe to his home. Abe and his parents lived in a beautiful home located near the crest of a hill overlooking the Pacific Ocean. Carl, on the other hand, was ashamed of his house and his neighborhood. The Spader family lived in the older section of San Diego, and their rented house was located midway up a steep hill stuffed between two other "shacks," as Carl called them. With the exception of Mike, the only person close to his age lived two blocks away, and was a girl. Not only were the houses in his neighborhood old, but so were most of the people who lived in them. No wonder they called it the "older" section of town.

The house was a simple square, weathered, wooden structure with a faded tile roof. The siding of the house was rain-stained gray with patches of sooty-white stucco trim. The slope of the land was such that the lower side of the house was ten feet lower in elevation than the upper side. A concrete retaining wall and chain-link fence seemed to be the only thing keeping the house from sliding down the hill.

The family had a miniscule front yard, and a stone and concrete barrier separated them from the narrow two-lane road that wound up the steep incline. Carl was grateful that it didn't snow in San Diego, or their vehicle could never navigate the steep hill. Their tiny backyard was barely big enough to contain a sand pile, a flowerbed, and two lawn chairs. The family didn't even own a garden hose. The entire yard, front and back, could be hand-watered once a week from a watering can.

If Carl walked twenty paces across the roadway, he could sit on the metal guardrail and look down on a crowded highway below. He could easily see the Marine Corps Recruit Depot and the Naval Training Center. When he watched the military and commercial planes arrive and leave, he envied those aboard. He figured he would never be able to afford to buy a ticket on an airplane.

Carl shifted positions in the small wooden chair and tried to organize his thoughts on how to start his story. So far, all he had done was fret about what a great life Abe had and how lousy his was. The only word on his paper was the first name of his friend.

Usually on Friday afternoons, Abe, Carl, and Mike would leave school together and do something for fun, but this particular day, Abe had been told by his mother to come directly home. Apparently, Dr. Stein had planned a weekend trip to Disneyland and wanted the family to get an early start on their drive to Anaheim. Abe had told Carl about the trip earlier that day, but Abe didn't sound very excited. It was one of those matter-of-fact comments. Abe and his family often spent their weekends away from home. Abe had been to Disneyland so many times he couldn't remember the number. Carl had been to Disneyland only once, two years earlier, and even that trip wouldn't have happened had it not been for his father's boss.

In regards to his second writing assignment, he could easily write about his Disneyland experience because it was not only his favorite vacation, it was his only vacation.

Bill's supervisor gave him four complimentary tickets to Disneyland. Bill questioned whether they should go, but it was Ruth who finally convinced him that the trip was important to the family. They had gone the following Sunday, the only day that Bill didn't work. It was the greatest event in the boy's life.

After a three-hour drive, they arrived at the Disneyland parking lot. Carl was so excited that his eyes were moist with tears of joy. When Bill realized that there was a charge to park, he whirled the car around and drove six blocks before he spotted a free parking spot. The walk back to the park was difficult for Bill, and the family had to make frequent rest stops. By the time they got to the entrance, the doors had been open a full hour, but it had saved one dollar.

The park was only three years old, having opened in 1955. It was immense and more than the brothers could have ever hoped for! The park was filled with music. There were replicas of turn-of-the-century houses and automobiles! It was a happy, mystical place with Disney characters and exciting whirling and tumbling rides! Carl could smell the newness of the park. Most of the trees and bushes were small, but that didn't matter to Carl because the park was marvelous, new, and exciting!

The complimentary package included park admission and ride tickets. The ride coupons were multicolored, varied in size, and were labeled with the letters *A* through *E*. Carl and Mike got to use the higher value *E* coupons because they were the ones that let them go on the more exciting wind-in-your-face rides. Bill's back couldn't take quick turns, so he confined his rides to the slow-moving attractions like the Mark Twain Paddle Wheel and the Disneyland Railroad. The rest of the family rode everything else. At noontime, Ruth brought out some rather compressed tuna sandwiches that she had carried all morning in her purse. With the aroma of hot dogs, hamburgers, mustard, and onions lingering in the air, the tuna sandwiches were rather disappointing, but it had saved them some money.

The family had a great time and hoped someday to repeat the experience, but it probably wouldn't happen because there simply wasn't enough money. There was never enough money.

Carl really liked Abe, but it was sometimes difficult for him to listen to his friend talk about all of the great things he and his parents had done and were planning to do together. Abe wasn't trying to make Carl feel bad nor was he trying to brag—it was just a fact of life.

A year earlier, Dr. Stein had included his parents (Abe's grandparents) on a two-week cruise. The cruise started at the docks in San Diego harbor and navigated along the Mexican coastline. Carl knew of at least three other cruises where Abe had been included.

Another time, on a Saturday evening, Dr. Stein had invited Bill and his family to go with them to the San Diego Zoo the next day. Dr. Stein explained to Bill that there would be no costs involved because a patient had given him four admission tickets, and he would be delighted to have the Spader family join them rather than have the tickets not be used. The Stein family didn't need tickets because every year they purchased annual family passes. Ruth waited in anxious anticipation for Bill's answer. When Bill reluctantly agreed, the family could hardly contain their joy.

Early the next morning the two families crowded into Dr. Stein's Packard automobile. It was the nicest car Carl had ever ridden in. Arriving at the zoo, Carl was impressed to see that there was a special parking place reserved for Dr. Stein, so the family only had to walk a few feet before entering the main gate.

Abe, Mike, and Carl took off on a run, not to be seen again until the scheduled meeting time of four o'clock. The four older people boarded a zoo transport bus, and although Dr. Stein, his wife, and Ruth did a lot of walking, Bill was content to sit on a park bench or ride and reride the zoo sightseeing bus.

After spending most of the day seeing thousands of animals, birds, and reptiles, the entourage all met at the scheduled place and time. Dr. Stein left his car in the parking stall, and the seven tourists walked to some nearby museums in Balboa Park. Dr. Stein had already made reservations for the group to see the outdoor stage production of *Brigadoon*. Bill tried to pay Dr. Stein for the tickets, but Dr. Stein told him that the tickets were perks for being a zoo annual pass holder. Abe was part of a marvelous family, and they weren't poor like Carl's.

Abe continued to invite Carl to go with him and his family on excursions. Dr. Stein even made a special point of letting Bill and Ruth know that he would cover the costs, but Bill's answer was always an unequivocal no. Bill Spader was simply too proud to accept the obvious charity. Dr. Stein eventually recognized the dilemma, and Abe, at his father's request, quit extending invitations.

Abe's weekends would continue to be grand. The Spader boys would most likely do things that wouldn't cost any money.

Bill worked evenings at his custodial job in an apartment complex located three blocks from their house. He left for work at three o'clock in the afternoon and didn't get home until after midnight. Except for Sundays, he rarely got to see the boys in the evenings. Ruth worked part-time on weekdays at a nearby nursing home.

Carl once overheard his father tell his mother, "I'm surprised that the military even accepted me, with only an eighth grade education." It was no wonder that his dad couldn't get a good-paying job. Carl was curious why his father hadn't wanted to finish high school. Someday he would build up enough courage to ask him.

Bill served in the army during World War II and had been seriously wounded. All Carl or Mike knew about the injury was that it impaired their father's ability to do hard work, participate in anything physical with his children, or stand in one place for long periods. They also knew that he had to be near a military veteran hospital. That was primarily the reason that his family had to remain in San Diego and weren't able to move to a less-expensive city.

The sound of footsteps on the porch jarred Carl back to reality. He had only written a few lines on the page when he heard the screen door bang shut. He shifted positions in the chair and tried once again to organize his thoughts. So far all he had done was reminisce about what a great life Abe had and how lousy a life was his own.

"We're home!" Ruth shouted as she entered the kitchen.

Carl rose from his chair and went to the kitchen to help Mike and his mother haul in the sacks of groceries.

The Spader family owned an old sun-faded Ford, but after dark, the vehicle had to be parked nearly a block from their home. They had no garage, and the street in front of their home didn't allow overnight parking. Mike and his brother made four trips to get in the stuff that Ruth had purchased, and then she drove the gas-guzzling oil burner to the vacant lot where it would be parked until eventually needed again. The rental space cost her two dollars a month.

Mike was back to his normal friendly self and greeted Carl with a sparring and jabbing ritual that was traditional between the brothers. Mike had an even, pleasant disposition, and although certainly not a wimp, he avoided verbal and physical confrontations. It was easy to see from physical appearance that Mike and Carl were brothers. Both had coloration and build similar to that of their father.

The brothers shared a small room housing two bunk beds. Mike, being younger, was relegated to the top bunk. There was one four-drawer dresser and a single rather warped mirror. They shared a table and a tiny clothes closet.

Both boys loved athletic events, and a wooden military footlocker stored their sporting equipment. Property was shared equally, and neither boy claimed ownership. Rarely was there a dispute, mostly because of Mike's good nature. Their inventory of sporting goods was sparse: a worn leather football with loose strings, a perpetually underinflated basketball, a softball bat, two scuffed baseballs, and two baseball gloves (purchase by Ruth at a garage sale for one buck).

Carl felt a little better after helping his mother and the three of them worked together to put away the groceries. Mike enthusiastically relayed the experiences of his day. Carl listened politely but certainly didn't share his jubilance of how his day had gone. He politely laughed at the proper time, but then he excused himself to finish his homework. Two hours later, he emerged from his bedroom with four of his six-page report completed. He wasn't proud of his work, but he knew he wasn't going to be held back a year because of it.

That evening, Ruth heated the last of their homemade vegetable soup. Cheese, fresh cool milk, and homemade bread completed the meal. After supper, the three of them adjourned to the living room. Ruth had access to the public library, and a five-cent bus ride coupled with a free library card took care of most of the family evening entertainment. She always tried to find books that would be interesting to young men, and then she would read them aloud. On the previous Thursday evening, she had finished the last chapter of a Louis L'Amour book. This evening she would start on a book of short stories written by Jack London.

As was the evening routine, Ruth sat on the couch between the boys. She had been born in England and spoke with a beautiful accent. Her sons loved the sound of her voice.

Brooms and Tanning Lotion

School would end next Monday afternoon, and then Carl would have the entire summer. It would remove a tremendous weight from his shoulders, if he could complete his homework assignment. He knew that he still had chores, but then on Tuesday his summer vacation would begin.

Saturday mornings were much the same, whether it was during the school year or the summer. Carl, Mike, and their mother got up early and devoted two hours to household chores. While their mother did the laundry, the boys shook the rugs, swept the carpet, and took out the garbage. No other activities would commence until their mother officially dismissed them. The best thing was that for most of the day, the family would be together. Even though Bill got home late on Friday night, he would generally get up early so he could spend time with his family. Today, the plan was to go to the beach. They would take a number 7 bus to Pacific Beach—their final destination.

With the house clean and the laundry done, the family assembled the necessities: a blanket, beach umbrella, fresh underwear, three bath towels, a picnic basket, and a cooler filled with ice water. Swimwear was worn under their clothing. Changing out of their damp swimsuits could be done in one of the free change houses. Bill never went into the water, and his sons never questioned why. Neither boy had ever seen their father in a swimming suit.

The family walked down the roadway to the bus stop. It cost five cents per person to ride, and it only took two transfers to get to the beach. The cost for the entire family never exceeded forty cents.

At the beach, the closest bus stop was four blocks from the water. Ruth and the boys divided the things they had brought from home and jogged ahead with Ruth close behind. Bill followed at a leisurely pace, armed only with his trusty beach chair tucked under his arm.

While Carl put up the umbrella, Ruth spread out the blanket and put the lunch and clothing shielded from the rays of the sun. She was considerate and careful to reserve a shady spot for Bill.

Ruth removed her wraparound while the boys shed their clothing down to their swim trunks. Since moving to San Diego, Ruth marked the traditional starting line in the sand. On the count of three, they all took off to sprint to the water's edge, and as usual, Ruth came in a distant third.

Several minutes later, Bill came into view, and his family waved gleefully. He waved back and then positioned his beach chair under the umbrella. He would stay in the same spot until it was time to go home. Mostly, he would just enjoy the activities of his family. Watching the clouds and surf seemed to bring him pleasure and contentment. The warmth of the sun, the sound of the ocean, and the gentle sea breeze would make him drowsy, and soon he would snooze. He wasn't interested in watching the girls on the beach. His mind would wander, obviously somewhere else far away.

It was a wonderful morning, and Carl concentrated on the enjoyment of the day rather than dwell on those luxuries in life that he and his family didn't have. The clan spent four hours on the beach before they were ready to eat lunch.

At noon they assembled under the umbrella to eat the peanut butter and jelly sandwiches and enjoyed drinking refreshing ice water. Talk was casual, and none of the family focused their conversation around lack of wealth or illness. The sun was high in the sky, and only a few fluffy clouds dotted the blue of the sky. The cool ocean breeze felt pleasant on their faces. After the last of the lunch was consumed, Mike took the accumulated trash and deposited into a nearby receptacle. When Mike returned, the three swimmers dashed into the ocean for one more dip before calling it a day. Bill remained under the umbrella and protected their possessions while his family showered and changed into dry clothing. When he saw them exit the change house, he smiled, waved, picked up his chair, and slowly and methodically walked toward the bus stop. The family knew where to meet him, and they knew he would not board the bus until all of his family had assembled. Bill would wait in the shade near the stop until his family arrived, and then they would depart together.

After making the ride to the stop nearest their home, they got off the bus and started the trek up the steep hill. The boys divided the beachwear, including Bill's chair, and raced each other to the top. Carl won by a few steps, but Mike was getting faster.

Ruth walked beside Bill, and they talked and laughed. She supported his elbow and assisted him as they meandered slowly, pausing often to let him stretch and massage his lower back.

Ruth had been successful in training the family members to remove their shoes before entering the house. It wasn't necessary on a regular day, but a trip to the beach carried with it added responsibilities.

At home Bill took a quick shower, shaved, and got into his sanitary white work clothes. Ruth handed him his sack lunch and gave him a peck on the cheek as he left for work. The boys hugged their father and walked part of the way with him before waving a friendly good-bye. The boys felt sad that their dad had to work six days a week. He always looked tired, but somehow he kept up such a good front. He continually joked and talked with the family. They truly loved their parents.

For the rest of the late afternoon, the boys played catch in their small backyard. They had to be careful not to errantly toss the ball too far, or it would clear the small boarder fence and roll clear to the highway at the bottom of the hill. They had never lost their ball, but on a few occasions, they spent considerable time trying to find it.

Ruth prepared a light meal of crackers, cheddar cheese, milk, and a slice of her wonderful homemade bread. After eating, the boys thundered across the floor as they raced each other to the bathroom, brushed their teeth, and got into their pajamas. The family then assembled in the living room where Ruth had already mixed up a pitcher of lemonade. Each family member found a favorite place to sit. Opening the book, Ruth selected a Jack London story and began to read. When it was either ten o'clock or when the boys' eyes started to roll and when the yawns appeared, whichever came first, it was time for them to go to bed.

Ruth chose a story about a man who got stranded in the cold and found shelter under a large pine tree. When the man was finally able to get a fire started, the heat from the fire melted some of the snow on the branches, and a pile of snow came crashing down on him and his fire. The story was captivating, and the boys listened intently to every word. Ruth, with her British accent, added flare to the story with her voice inflections.

Mike was the first to yawn, and that seemed to be contagious because Carl yawned just seconds later. All three of the family members laughed. The boys obediently kissed their mother and headed off to their room on a run. They seemed to always want to race, regardless of the distance.

Sunday morning was another beautiful day, commonplace in San Diego. Bill was the first to get up and was relaxing in his pajamas at the kitchen table when Ruth exited the bathroom.

"Good morning, sweetheart," Ruth greeted.

Bill smiled and muttered a similar greeting.

The couple sat at the table for several minutes just looking at each other, neither feeling a need to talk. Each loved the other with all of their hearts, and neither needed to be verbally reminded of that love.

The contemplative moment was interrupted with the sound of a morning pillow fight between the boys. Ruth and Bill smiled at each other, and both simultaneously shook their heads.

"Breakfast will be served in thirty minutes, so you two get washed and ready for church!" Ruth shouted.

The family took turns using the bathroom, and after eating some Quaker Oats mush, as Bill called it, the family left their home and walked the short distance to attend their local church.

The meeting was enjoyable, and the preacher talked about how everyone should be grateful for all of their blessings and to avoid coveting the possessions of another. Carl looked at his parents' expressions to see if they were showing any particular emotions to what the preacher had just said, there was none. On the other hand, Carl could hardly contain himself on the bench. All he ever thought about was how little he and his family had and how much the Stein family had. By the end of the meeting, Carl was feeling so guilty that he avoided shaking hands with the preacher when they exited the church building.

The walk home was casual and relaxed. Both Ruth and Bill sensed Carl's concerns and avoided talking about the church message.

Ruth prepared a macaroni and cheese casserole for their lunch, and when they were all through eating, Bill went to the bedroom to take a short nap. Carl and Mike sat on the living room floor and played checkers. If they had owned a TV, they would probably have watched a ball game or an old Western movie, but that would have to wait until the day when, or if, they could ever afford to purchase such a luxury item.

Carl couldn't put his finger on it, but he was still uneasy and frustrated. He was full of self-pity, and the preacher's sermon hadn't done anything to help his attitude. He seldom quarreled with Mike, but this particular evening, practically everything his brother did or said was annoying to Carl. Carl didn't like the way Mike sat, or his delay in making his checker moves, or the way Mike quietly snickered if Carl made a poor move. Mike was also getting a little irritated and was keenly aware that his brother wasn't acting like his normal self.

When Bill entered the living room, the boys eagerly put away the game. Bill slowly sat down in his favorite chair, propped himself with pillows, and then Ruth finished reading the few remaining pages from the previous evening. She paused only long enough to let the family briefly discuss the story before starting the next story. It was a tale about a relationship that existed between a young Eskimo boy and his grandfather. Ruth had read only a few pages when Carl was reminded of his school assignment to write a story about his own grandparents. That recollection seemed to stir something deep inside him because he jumped to his feet and interrupted his mother in midsentence. Carl had a frown on his face, and he spoke loudly.

"I have been with Abe's grandparents, and often they talk about different things that have happened in their lives. Last Sunday I heard Grandpa Stein tell a story about when he and his wife arrived in America with only forty dollars between them.

Look at the money they have now! Grandpa Stein is rich, and so are his three sons. I enjoy hearing those stories, but all I know about my grandparents is that they are all dead. I know nothing about your early lives. Are you ashamed to tell me about them? Were they murderers or spies?"

Mike's mouth dropped open, and he was stunned and flabbergasted at Carl's outburst.

Carl continued his assault. "Members of the Stein family have big, beautiful homes, they drive new cars, and they go on vacations—all the time. We don't have nothin'!" Still not finished, Carl directed his pent-up wrath toward his father. "Abe's father is a doctor. You are a janitor. Why didn't you try to improve yourself so things would be better for us? Why didn't you at least finish high school? Why is your health so bad? Didn't you take care of yourself?"

Carl loved his parents, and he knew that they loved him. He couldn't even begin to explain his behavior. He got started, and the more he talked, the more things he found to complain about. Turning to his mother, he said, "I know that you lived with your parents in England. You are a nurse and clean up the messes caused by elderly people." And then to his father, "I think that your parents lived and died in Idaho or somewhere in the west. That's the sum total of what I know about my grandparents."

The more Carl rambled, the more explosive his speech became. His disappointment and agony of being poor was overriding any desire he might have had to spare hurting his parents' feelings. His face was red, tears flowed from his eyes, and often his voice cracked, but he continued unabashed.

Ruth was getting visibly upset, and she jumped to her feet, about to plow into Carl and set him straight, but Bill held up his hand, gently shook his head, and gestured with a finger to his lips for her to stay her comments.

"Go ahead, son. This is getting good," Bill said. Ruth just looked at her husband in disbelief.

Carl continued his verbal attack. "You are a janitor! We can barely live, and Mother has to work! Our car is a ten-year-old Ford disgrace, and it is only used in an emergency because it puts out blue smoke and uses too much gas and oil. The makeshift clunker air-conditioning that someone installed doesn't work, and Mike and I have to always ride in back where the windows only roll partway down! We have to put an old horse blanket on the seat because the upholstery is full of holes, and the springs protrude! Our only vacation in our lives was the one to Disneyland two years ago, and that's because someone else gave you the tickets. If it hadn't been for a few free outings sponsored by the school,

Mike and I wouldn't have gone anywhere fun!" Carl ended by bursting into tears and flopping angrily back onto the couch.

Ruth and Mike were stunned, and Bill didn't answer immediately. He put three fingers to his lips, silently pondering what had just been said. Slowly he stood and motioned for Mike to exchange seating positions with him. Bill sat down next to his eldest son, placed his arm around his shoulders, and pulled him close. Bill held him for a long time as Carl sobbed. Neither said anything.

"Carl, I know you have been suffering, and so have we. Life hasn't been as good to us as we would have liked, but we have to live with what we are given. The main reason we live here in San Diego rather than a less-expensive city is because I need to be near the military hospital. Son, I thought that the monthly disability check from the government would be sufficient to cover our extra costs, but it simply isn't. Your mother and I do the best we can, but it is difficult, and you have every right to say what you think. I am certainly not angry with you. San Diego has a wonderful climate with lots of things to do, but because it is so nice, many people want to live here, and that is also one of the reasons why it is such an expensive place. It probably won't help to share all of the particulars of how I got us into this fix, but I will try. I am not insensitive to your concerns, and probably the one thing we can do is to answer your questions about your grandparents and ourselves. We should have done that a long time ago, but I guess we were just too busy or maybe just unaware of your concerns. To you and Mike, I apologize for that. You two go use the bathroom, get yourselves a glass of lemonade, and your mother and I will bore you to death with our life stories." Bill finished talking and hugged Carl and roughed up his sandy hair.

Carl immediately felt horrible about his outburst and started to apologize to his parents.

Bill cut him off. "We should have talked to you. We just weren't paying enough attention to your concerns."

Laughter and Tears

"Requesting a person to summarize ones life is like asking someone the length of a piece of string. We can tell you about an event in just a few minutes, but a life story is not a short story," Ruth said. "Now where do you want us to start, and what is it exactly that you want to know?"

Carl gave the question some thought, and then answered. "I want to know about each of your childhoods, what you did for fun. Who were your friends? I want to know more about you and father. I want to be able to tell my own children, when I have them, about their grandparents and great-grandparents. What I want to do Mom—is to know more about you than that you cook, sew, work in a nursing home, and read books to me." Carl continued. "Most of my friends eat Sunday dinner with their grandparents. They sit in the living room and listen to stories about a time before there were was television, wide highways, powerful cars, and electric toasters. Did your parents ride in a buggy pulled by a horse? Were they ever wealthy, or were they as poor as we are? Mom, I want to know what it means to be part of them!"

Bill and Ruth looked at each other as if trying to determine who should speak first. Ruth finally broke the silence. "Well, let me start. My story is going to be shorter than that of your father. He has never been able to tell a short story." Bill just shrugged his shoulder, raised the skin on his forehead, and rolled his eyes in agreement

Ruth continued. "When I was only twelve years old, I once asked my mother almost exactly the same question that you just asked us. I knew nothing about my parent's lives. She didn't provide me with an immediate answer, and it took my sweet mother a full week to finish and present me with a little notebook. It contained a handwritten record of her life. It includes historical data about my father's birth, work, and things like that, but it also gave my mother's insight regarding the qualities that my father possessed. It is priceless to me, and is the one item that I still have from the family of my youth. I value it above my other possessions—I cherish it. Do you understand what I am telling you? If either of you ever want to read it, you may do so, but not without my permission."

Ruth stood and walked into her bedroom. She opened a cabinet door and took out a small, hand-carved decorated wooden chest. Returning, she sat between Bill and Carl on the couch. She didn't open the container immediately, just looked at it fondly as if deciding in her own mind whether she wanted to share the contents. She looked at Carl, and touched his cheek with the back of her soft hand. Her eyes were moist, and her hands were trembling as she opened the lid with such care that one would have thought it contained fragile crystal.

"Once I start, I want to finish. I don't want to be interrupted because this is hard for me to read. Do you fully understand what I am telling you?" she asked.

"I understand Mom," Carl replied. Mike nodded his head.

Bill moved slowly back to his chair and motioned with his head for Mike to sit next to his mother. Ruth patted a place next to her and Mike sat down. She began.

"What I am going to read to you was written by my dear mother many years ago. It is an account of her family history, and in reading it, I gained an insight into the lives of my parents and grandparents. It is like a diary or journal. I will read the document exactly as it was written twenty-four years ago. Since the information is dated, I will also read to you the date so you will know when the event happened. Also notice that the language is not necessarily the same way we speak now, nor is it the way you are being taught in school."

It was on a Saturday, the first day of June in 1934 when Ruth, my twelve year-old-daughter, asked me to tell her about my life, and the lives of my parents. I will write down what I can remember. Much of my story comes from my own diary and from newsprint articles.

"My name is Elna Glover Clay, and I was born in Copenhagen, Denmark on January 5, 1882. My parents were Jacob Glover and Enid Nielsen. Three children were born to them, but I was the only one that lived more than five days.

"My childhood was spent on a farm a few miles from Copenhagen. My father was a constable [policeman]. My mother, Enid Nielsen, was educated in Copenhagen. She completed two years of college and was one of the first women to be licensed to teach in a high school. My father was in law enforcement at the time, and he was summoned to the school where she worked to investigate the disappearance of several coats missing from a clothing rack.

"My mother's coat was among those missing. Jacob conducted a thorough investigation, but seemed to take a considerable interest in Enid's coat. He returned several times to collect specific information that he said he had previously overlooked or needed to investigate further. One time it was the specific color, the next visit would require more information pertaining to the lining and the type of fabric, another time it was a description of the collar. Jacob was a sly one, he was.

"Mother didn't mind and that was the start of a wonderful relationship. Jacob did eventually find the coats and they were returned to their owners. He personally delivered Enid's coat to her. In the pocket he placed a pressed flower inside a small book of poetry. Naturally he included a note letting Enid know the name of the sender.

"The romance continued to grow, and after a two-year engagement, they got married in 1880.

A constable's pay was barely adequate to cover the needs of a family, so he supplemented his income by milking cows. He took out a bank loan guaranteed by his uncle, and by working mornings and late evenings he soon had enough money to pay off all of his debts and buy six more cows. The farm became their livelihood and Jacob resigned his job as constable.

Most of the milk collected was used to make cheese. Each dairy farmer was part of a co-op, and farmers received money based upon the pounds of cheese that were sold. If a dairy farmer contributed ten percent of the milk, then he got back ten percent of the profits.

It was a difficult life with long hours, and our family seldom had free time. We occasionally got together with neighbors or rode in the wagon into the city, but I don't recall my childhood as being much fun—mostly work.

It was cold where we lived, so we had to wear coats or sweaters nearly all year. We raised most of our own food, but the winters were long and the growing season was limited. Often our crops would freeze before they could ever be harvested.

I stayed on the farm for a long time, but I hated cows. What I wore, ate, or touched smelled like cows. I loved my parents, but I hated the dairy. I wanted to meet a nice fellow, fall in love, get married, and have children.

In regards to my own life, I felt like I was an 'old maid' at seventeen when I packed my bags, gave my parents a hug and a kiss and moved into town. I got a job washing dishes in an eatery where my meals were provided. Now, having my own money, I paid a modest rent and bought my clothing. That job lasted two years before the building burned to the ground. The owner never rebuilt. Without so much as a word to any of us, he loaded his remaining belongings into his wagon and drove away.

I was able to find new work at another eatery; this time I was hired as a waitress, and my meals were still included. It was while working at the diner, that I met Henry Clay.

I learned some time later that Henry's father had died when Henry was only fourteen years old. He was the eldest son, so he had to accept the responsibility of being the breadwinner for the family. To earn money, he quit school and signed a three-year contract to be a cabin boy on a fishing vessel. He cleaned cabins, decks, fish, and mended nets. He sent most of his pay back to support his widowed mother, but she died just two years after he had lost his father.

By the age of twenty-one, Henry was an accomplished fisherman, and had traveled all over the world. He was loyal, and he still worked on the same vessel he had started with seven years earlier. He was now First Mate. He was fair, talented, respected, and he knew the sea. He also had a knack of getting along with even the most cantankerous and toughest of men.

While in port in Copenhagen, Henry and several other seamen were given a one-week shore leave while their boat was being overhauled and scraped for barnacles. The crew's first stop was to find lodging, and after they stowed their gear, they went looking for good food and ale. Henry and his crew happened to come into the eatery one afternoon. I had been working there for only two months. I was one of two barmaids, and the crew from the ship sat at one of the table that was assigned to me.

Henry and I exchanged glances and I liked what I saw. Maybe it was because he was tall and broad and had a trim beard and a strong jaw, but I thought I detected something else, maybe a spark of interest on his part too. Each time I turned around, he would be looking right at me—always smiling showing his pearly-white teeth. He was really quite handsome if I do say so me self!

It didn't take his friends long to notice our mutual attraction. They started whispering and poking him in his ribs. I had been aware of most events that happened at his table. Once, Henry made some funny comment and out of the corner of my eye I saw him wave his hands to emphasize his story. His shipmates laughed heartily and I impulsively turned.

Looking toward him and walking forward with a heavy platter of dirty dishes was a poor decision. I didn't watch where I was going, and stumbled on the leg of a heavy oak chair. I lost my balance but didn't fall. What I did do, however, was to drop the tray of dirty dishes directly into the middle of a nearby table. Fortunately, no one was sitting there. Just a few minutes earlier I had finished setting the table with pewter, mugs, and silverware.

My accident caused a terrible noise, and it just kept going on! One of the metal plates would clank to the floor, then a spoon or fork. Next a mug would roll off the table onto the hardwood floor. I reached to catch another metal mug before it fell, but when I did I knocked over the flower arrangement positioned in the middle of the table. Patrons jumped at the initial noise, but then they started to laugh as the noise of my errors just kept coming. There was nothing I could do, so I just stood back, put my hands on my hips and waited for the dishes to quit falling and the noise to stop. They all knew it was an accident, but it was rather funny to them. There was no real harm because nothing broke. I am confident that many of them had had similar experiences.

My employer saw, and obviously heard, what had happened. He was embarrassed and shouted loudly and angrily at me. I felt badly, but in his wrath, he told me, "Elna Glover, you are fired!"

There weren't many jobs available at that time, and I needed that job. When he fired me, my world suddenly fell apart. I was embarrassed, distraught, and angry all at the same time. I glared at my boss and then threw my apron on the table and ran into the street. I was shaking and crying, and I had to lean against the outside wall to keep from swooning.

Then a rather strange thing happened. The handsome young man at my table came running out of the door and stopped next to me. He politely introduced himself as Henry Clay, and told me he would be right back. He instructed me to stay where I was. I was too dumbstruck to do anything else, so I stayed right where he told me to stay.

I could see what was going on through a side window of the eatery. This tall man [Henry] walked back inside and went directly to my employer. He stood to his full height of six feet four inches and puffed out his chest. In his deepest, strongest voice, Henry bellowed at the man loudly enough for all in the establishment to hear. I knew they could hear, because I was outside, and I could certainly hear.

Henry told the man that he had never in his life seen a worse display of rudeness to an employee. He informed the man that he was the spokesman for a large number of seafaring men who frequented the Copenhagen eating establishments. Henry assured my employer that he would do his utmost to convince all seamen to never patronize this particular eatery.

It wasn't until later that I found out that Henry had no such authority or title, but my employer sure thought he did. I will always remember Henry's exact words:

"We here in this room [he theatrically swept his arms around to include everyone] all believe in the sanctity of womanhood. Any man who does not share that respect is most certainly not deserving of our patronage. Good day to you, sir!"

Henry took out a fistful of currency and coins, and without even counting it, he dropped the entire amount clinking onto the center of his table.

I knew that Henry and the other members of his party were almost through eating, so the gesture wasn't going to cause them to leave hungry. His seaman friends had obviously caught on to what he was doing, because each of them stood in mock disgust and thrust down their money on the table.

Others in the pub were startled and caught off guard. They didn't know how to react, but each somehow thought it must be the proper thing to do, so one by one they stood and threw their fares onto their tables. My hero headed for the door and most of the other patrons in the diner followed after him.

Henry told me later that even he was surprised at the mass exodus. A few of the patrons hadn't even started to eat their meals, but to his surprise, they followed him when he left the eatery. "My use of the word 'womanhood' must have struck a tender cord with them," he later told me.

Through the window I could see the owner's face turning pale and his hands and lower lip was trembling. He was panicked and could see his whole business crumbling right in front of his eyes! The owner raced to the door to get in front of Henry before he and the others left. He pleaded for Henry to forgive him. He was almost in tears.

"I was in error and wasn't thinking clearly. It was the wrong thing to do, and I truly apologize. How can I make this right?" the man pleaded. Again Henry put his nose right up next to that of the owner. He paused for several seconds before speaking.

Again I want to quote Henry as accurately as I can remember: "You find that lovely lady, whom you just publicly humiliated. Beg her forgiveness. Offer her higher pay, a bonus, or what you must. You had better convince her to come back. If she is willing to return, and to again work for someone as wretched as you, then I will forget this incident ever happened. I am sure the others here would be in agreement with me."

His shipmates nodded grimly, and that made the others who had been in the room feel compelled to nod their heads also. My employer looked so relieved. He raced past Henry into the street.

Witnessing the conversation inside, I was prepared when I saw my employer head toward the door. Before he saw me, I started walking, head down, slowly and dejectedly. I dabbed at my eyes with my kerchief, and added to the effect by dropping my shoulders.

I heard his footsteps on the street's cobblestones, and I knew my employer was getting close. I actually had to cover my mouth with my kerchief to keep from laughing. Then, there he was! He raced to be in front of me. Shaking, and with tears in his eyes, he begged for my forgiveness. I kept walking forward, but he stayed in front of me, while walking backwards. He offered me a bonus and more pay. He opened his purse and tried to force money into my hands. He again pleaded with me to return. I finally stopped and he gently forced open my clenched fist and filled it with money. He grasped both my hands and kissed them. Again he begged for me to forgive him for his unjust treatment.

[Being the type of forgiving person I was and with tongue in cheek], I relented and returned rather reluctantly to the eatery with him. He opened the door for me. The few patrons inside the establishment applauded my return. Just a few minutes earlier I had been fired—now I was being treated like royalty. I picked up my soiled apron but, before I could put it on, my employer gently removed it from my hand. Suddenly he was all smiles and politeness.

"I will take care of this, you go back with your customers!" he said.

All of the patrons in the pub were standing, and when they realized the problem had been resolved, those who had left with Henry returned to their seats. The buzzing in the eatery started again, and soon everyone was eating his or her somewhat cooler food. Henry and his fellow seaman sat down and enjoyed a leisurely cup of tea.

When the eatery closed that evening, I was given an envelope containing the equivalent of one week's pay. I was told that my pay rate was being increased, and that I could take the next day off, with pay. The tips I received from the patrons that day were greater than I had ever received before.

This Henry was quite a person to know!

After the eatery closed, I started my walk home. Who just happened to be waiting for me under a lamppost? It was my big lovable Henry.

As I approached where he was standing, he smiled and asked me if he could walk me home. I assured him that I was honored.

From that time until Henry's shore leave was over, we spent all of our available days together. Henry was a Scot through and through and he could understand me better than I could understand him. It took me several years before I caught each word that Henry said to me.

Henry hadn't had much formal schooling, but he was honorable and intelligent. He spent much of his free time reading books and improving his mind. He was good at math and had memorized many passages of scripture as well as pieces of poetry. He had traveled to so many places that he was an authority on geography as well as history. My Henry was a pretty smart fella', he was! After he shipped out, we wrote letters to each other and got together and each time he came to Copenhagen.

When I was working in the eatery, Henry would come in and purchase his meals. I always served him, and my employer treated Henry like he was his favorite customer and best friend. Neither Henry nor I ever even considered divulging our deception. It took two long years of letters and courting before I accepted Henry's proposal of marriage. It wasn't that I didn't want to get married it was that my Henry simply had cold feet. It took him that long to build up enough courage to ask.

He didn't know it, but I would have accepted his marriage proposal that first night under the lamppost if he had asked. I knew all I needed to know about the man, and I had already made up my mind that he was the one for me. He was a 'gonna' be my husband, even if he didn't know it yet.

We were married on the last day of June, 1903, in Edinburgh, Scotland. My parents were still alive, but weren't able to attend the wedding because it was so far from their home in Denmark. Of course, Henry's parents had died several years earlier, so we had no blood relatives to celebrate the event with us.

We lived in Edinburgh for twenty-one years until 1924 when we moved to London, England.

Henry continued working on the fishing vessel, but the long intervals between our times together was difficult for him and for me. We had no way of communicating while he was at sea, and often he would be gone for three months at a time. Henry kept a log of what happened while he was away, and I kept a journal of what was happening in my life. For some reason we had never been able to have children although we both wanted some. Then, when I was thirty-nine years old, and only days after Henry left for sea, I found out that I was pregnant with our first child. It was March, 1922, and Henry didn't get the good news until he came home in early May. I got a letter from him in April letting me know that he would be home within a few weeks. The letter was short, and his penmanship wasn't as refined as normal. I sensed that something was wrong even though there was no mention of it in the letter. There was no return address, so I couldn't write back. Since I never knew exactly when his boat would arrive in port, I was unable to meet him at the dock.

One afternoon, Henry just showed up with a sea bag flung over his right shoulder. I could see that his left hand was bandaged and his arm was in a sling.

I had been busy making bread in our small flat when I heard his footsteps on the cobblestone. It was a chilly day, but I had the window open to let in the afternoon breeze and to freshen up the room. I dropped my apron on the kitchen floor and raced to the street to meet him. I was concerned about his injury, but Henry just waved off my question.

We spent the rest of the afternoon and evening talking and holding one another. His sea bag was full of gifts and souvenirs that he had purchased in Sweden, Holland, and Norway. I was overjoyed at the items he had purchased. We laughed and enjoyed each other's reaction as the trinkets were examined—each item had a story of its own.

It was at this time that I told him that he was going to be a father. Henry burst into tears. We had both given up the idea of children, and suddenly our prayers had been answered. He kept asking me if it was going to be a boy and I kept telling him that I had no idea. Then, every few minutes he would repeat the question. We enjoyed that time together. It was just before we went to bed that I was finally able to convince Henry that he should tell me how he got hurt.

Henry explained that the Captain of his fishing vessel had located a large school of herring. The number of fish was so plentiful that the men worked frantically until they were physically and mentally exhausted. One of the nets got entangled under the boat and a sailor was dispatched to dislodge the snare. The man was successful in freeing the net, but as he climbed back up the wooden and rope ladder, he slipped on one of the rungs and fell backwards into the icy water. The water in the channel between Norway and England is frigid cold, and the man had drifted several feet from the vessel. He had to be rescued immediately before his body temperature dropped to a critical point. Henry was forward when he heard the shouting. He raced aft and threw a tethered life preserver into the water near the sailor. The sailor clung to the preserver while several of the men aboard pulled him closer to the boat. Henry climbed down the wet ladder to help. After numerous attempts, he was finally successful in grasping the frightened man and pulling him close to the ladder. The sailor was so cold that he could barely grip the ladder rung and he had essentially no strength left in his legs. Henry clutched the man around the waist and used all of his strength to hoist the sailor up the ladder. Near the top, as the near frozen man was being lifted over the railing, the wooden rung under Henry's foot snapped under the weight of the two men. Henry wildly grasped for a handhold on the ladder and instantaneously felt a sharp pain in his left wrist and he let out a scream. An alert seaman grabbed Henry's coat and held tightly until other crewmen could hoist him aboard. Wrapped in blankets, he was rushed to the Captain's cabin and stretched out on the bunk.

When Henry fell, he must have grabbed the rope ladder near where the wooden rung had shattered. The splintered end of the rung, still attached snugly to the rope, had impaled Henry's wrist and momentarily held him from falling. Fragments of the wood were lodged in Henry's left wrist and protruded out of the palm of his hand. There was nothing to ease Henry's pain and he swooned as the jagged six-inch splinter was extracted. Immediately the Captain thrust a knife into the glowing coals in his cabin stove. At the same time, a sailor poured rum into the entry and exit wounds and stuffed cloth into the holes to stop the severe bleeding. Henry nearly passed out when the injury was cauterized with the red-hot knife. He wobbled as he was assisted to his own cabin and placed on his bunk. The Captain covered him with blankets and stoked up the pot-bellied stove. A sailor was assigned to stay by Henry's bunk that entire evening to make sure the wound didn't start bleeding again.

The next day Henry dressed and tried to perform his duties, but the pain was so severe that he was ineffective. Over the next two days Henry's condition worsened. His wrist doubled in size and his hand and wrist had to be lanced on two separate occasions to drain the infection. He was feverish, drenched in perspiration and shuddered with severe chills when the Captain made the decision to head back to England. The trip took three more days, and by the time the vessel docked at Southampton, Henry was unconscious and rambling. A doctor was summoned and Henry was transported to a hospital. The next morning the doctor performed surgery to remove remnants of the wood splinter, and to repair the extensive damage to his wrist and hand. The surgery took six hours, and Henry was kept in the hospital for three more days. On the fourth day, when Henry's fever had dropped to normal, the doctor sat by his bed and gave him the bad news.

I read what Henry wrote in his journal and I have included that portion in mine exactly as written. The doctor told Henry. "Henry my boy, you have sustained a serious injury, and the tendons and nerves in your wrist and hand have been extensively damaged. You have lost a lot of blood, and you are very weak from the ordeal you have been through. The holes in your wrist and hand will heal well through time, but you have lost your ability to firmly grasp anything with your left hand. You will never again get back the strength you once had--the strength necessary to be a commercial fisherman. The nerve damage has left the left side of your hand numb, and that feeling will most likely never return. As much as I hate to tell you, my son, your seafaring days are over."

My eyes were moist and my hands trembled as I held Henry's face in my hands. It was obvious that he didn't want to talk more about his injury, and I respected his wishes. I cradled him in my arms and stroked his face and hair for an hour before we finally retired. He was restless during the night and didn't sleep well, partially because of pain, but mostly because of his uncertainty about what the future held for us.

The next morning, he stayed in our room for a long time, but when he finally came out of the bathroom, he had a big smile on his face.

"Elna" he said, "I have done some real soul-searching, and I have made a decision! I am going to deliver mail! With a job like that, it will let me get some fresh air and will let me be home at night with my family. I am going to be the best postman that ever roamed the streets of London!"

Henry did get his job as a postman and we started anew.

Furthermore, we were blessed with two daughters, Ruth and Emily. Ruth was born on October 5, 1922, and Emily arrived December 1, 1924.

My husband, Henry Clay was born on January 10, 1880 in Edinburgh, Scotland to George Clay and Gwenice Green Clay. George died of pneumonia in 1894, at age 35, when Henry was only fourteen years old.

Henry's mother was born in Edinburgh, Scotland in 1860, and died of pneumonia in 1896 at age 36.

> Ruth interjected. "Remember, I was twelve years old when she wrote this. My parents died five years later.
>
> Ruth got out of her high-back chair, made a short trip to the bathroom, then to the kitchen where she soon came back with four glasses and a large ice laden pitcher of lemonade. Each of the family members filled their respective glass and settled back into their seats. Ruth was now ready to begin her story. Leaning forward, she paused, took a sip of her lemonade, took a deep breath, smiled at her husband and boys, and then spoke.

"I was born on a Thursday morning in Edinburgh, Scotland on October 5, 1922—the same day, month, and year as your father. My father was Henry Clay and my mother was Elna Glover Clay. I was given the name of Ruth Clay (no middle name or initial). I remember nothing of my early years in Scotland, because I was just a two-year old child and we moved from Edinburgh to London. My mother was pregnant with Emily, and my sister was born just two months after we moved into our new flat. My first memory of my early life in London was when my parents took my sister and me to see the Changing of the Guard at Buckingham Palace. I think I was about six or seven years old at the time. It was so impressive with the beautiful horses and the splendidly uniformed men who marched so straight and tall. I have seen that event repeated many times since, but that first time is my most vivid memory.

"When I was eight, all of my family rode the train to Stonehenge. We took a picnic basket and ate our lunch with our backs wedged against the tall massive rocks that encircled us. My father told me the story about how he thought the stones were brought there, but none of those memories are still with me. With each subsequent telling of the story, the method of transportation changes depending upon who is telling the story.

"In London, we had 'Bobbies,'—our English name for policemen, and most of them rode horses and wore mustaches. Our conveyances were referred to as 'carriages' rather than automobiles. It wasn't until I married your father that we saved enough money to purchase an automobile. In London we rode exclusively in Cabbies because they were always available for hire if we needed to go somewhere. We didn't live in apartments—we lived in 'flats'.

"I received my early education in an 'all-girls' school located only a few buildings away from where we lived. It was a joyful time for me. I had many friends and we used to run through the halls and play 'hide-and-seek' in the various rooms, nooks and crannies. The dormitory was four stories tall and had hundreds of windows. One of our chores was to clean the inside of the window glass, and we all hated it. The building was heated by two large coal furnaces, and it seemed like as much soot came into the building as went out the chimney. Our clothing always smelled of smoke and mold.

"I was intrigued when the men who were all dressed in black clothing and wearing tall dark hats arrived. They were called 'Chimney Sweeps', and when summoned by our building superintendent, these men came to clean and repair the smokestacks. They were so agile! They climbed up their long ladders and gracefully hopped around on the roof like a bunch of monkeys! They were filthy, and one could barely see their eyes because their faces were so covered with soot and ash, but they always seemed to be happy.

"We weren't involved much in sporting and athletic events. We played with dolls, skipped rope, and did a lot of dancing, mostly ballet. Until I was fourteen we girls dressed in identical blue and white uniforms. We looked more like sailors than students! We wore funny round, uncomfortable bonnets with a red bow on the brow of our cap. When we ran fast or jostled with one another, the large bow would bounce forward and cover our eyes so we couldn't see. We wore long black stockings, black slips, and checkered skirts. Our blouses were white, but we had a bright red vest—the same color as the bow on our bonnet. There was an emblem—like a coat-of-arms on our vests, but it was the crest of our school, not our family crest.

Our teachers were stiff and stern, and it seemed to me that all of them were over ninety and must have been trained to never smile. We had to be very formal and call them by their surnames—Miss Dabney, Miss Oborn, or Miss Knight. I don't know if any of them were married—they never wore makeup or jewelry. Their black dresses covered their entire bodies except for their hands and faces. They wore a black lace neck collar that seemed to hold their chins up. They carried long pointer sticks, and more than once I felt that stick crack down on my knuckles or bottom when they thought I had done something wrong. I tried to be a good student, mainly because I knew I needed to have good grades if I wanted to be a nurse or a teacher. The rebellious or unruly girls also seemed to be the ones who got the poorer grades and the most punishment.

My sister Emily and I were always close, and although we were in different classes, we created opportunities to meet one another during the school day, but most of our time together came after school and on the weekends. My best classmate friend was a girl named Irma. We studied together, played 'hopscotch', dressed-up, and read mystery and romance novels. Irma folded the corners of pages where the more 'spicy' parts of a book could be found. An inch thick book was generally had grown much larger at the corners when Irma got through with it!

"We both liked boys but we didn't know many. Occasionally, my school would sponsor a dance. Teachers would bring boys to our school and act as chaperones. We would get a chance to dance, drink punch, eat cookies, and flirt a little. We looked forward to that."

Ruth continued with her story and ignored Carl and Mike while they giggled.

"We lived in a tall building that housed many families. Few people owned houses, and most of those who did were farmers living on the outskirts of the city. We had neither a lawn nor a garden, so my father built some planter boxes from old shipping crates that had been discarded and left on the docks. Our flat faced east, and there was a planter box on every windowsill so that it would face the morning sun. Mother raised mostly plants that we could eat—cucumbers and tomatoes, but she mixed in flowers for aroma and beauty. It was my job to keep the plants watered, but often I had to be reminded of my duties. Up until the time I married your father, watering those plants represented the sum total of my farming skills! I lived in London with my parents and Emily until I was fifteen years old. We had very little money, but we were happy.

"A major conflict between England and Germany was feared by many people at that time, so in 1937 my father and mother made the decision to send me to Scotland to go to school. Because my father was a native Scot and I had been born there, I was permitted to enroll even though I was currently living in England. My parents were very happy that I was out of harm's way.

"I was excited about nursing, and my biggest desire in life was to be a nurse. The high school in Scotland made provisions for a student to concurrently specialize in a trade or profession. With this opportunity, I got my education but also learned all that I could about caring for the ill and the elderly. In spite of being homesick, my time in Scotland was wonderful! I got a part-time job working in a bakery, and the supervisor taught me how to bake pastry and cook meat pies. I also got to be a pretty good cake decorator!

"Whenever I wasn't in school, I was reading about nursing. I volunteered to work at a local hospital and learned how to care for wounds, tie bandages, assist doctors, and care for children, sick people, and the elderly. I did take time to see Scotland, but most of it was by foot, bus, or cycle. I loved the beauty of the country! I adored the sound of the people's voices because they so reminded me of my father! As you all know, I have an English accent and somehow never acquired the Scottish brogue of my father.

"There was a shortage of petrol [gasoline], so most of my travel was on foot or cycle. We all had to know how to patch tires, because there were no new ones available. I had many friends—boys and girls, and we spent most of our evenings and weekends on trails or paths. I learned a lot about the country of my birth, and was becoming a proud Scot.

I was seventeen, and living in a school dormitory when I received a letter that changed my life forever. It was from one of our London neighbors, Mrs. Barker. She tried to be delicate in her letter, but from her I learned that my family had all been killed, and it was devastating to me. London was being bombed almost every night, and one of the dreadful German bombs fell onto the building where we lived. There was a terrible explosion and subsequent fire, and many people were injured, but amazingly, only five people in the entire building were killed, but among those were my parents and my sister Emily. I fell on the couch and wept, and I really don't remember much of what happened over those next few days. Only pieces of their bodies and clothing were even found so no formal burial services were held. My parents and sister must have been directly under the bomb when it hit, so I believe that they didn't suffer. I was encouraged in Mrs. Barker's letter to stay in Scotland where it was safe. I said a lot of prayers on behalf of my family, and my friends were supportive and gave me comfort during those hard times."

It took a few minutes before Ruth could regain her composure. Carl's eyes were also filled with tears, and he felt badly that he had encouraged his mother to share such a difficult memory. A few more minutes passed, and then Ruth looked at Carl and Michael, managed a faint smile, dabbed at her eyes with her kerchief and continued.

"I spent the next four years completing my education. In 1943, I returned to London, but this time as a licensed nurse. That is where I met this lug!" She pointed at Bill. "He got himself all shot-up in France in 1944. The army shipped him to our London military hospital and I nursed him back to health, but he can tell you about that.

"The war was still going strong, but your father's injuries were very serious, and the doctors said is was highly unlikely that he would be sent back into combat. He had served valiantly and came home as a decorated war hero. It wasn't until much later that I learned he had been wounded once before I met him, but his second injury is the one that required my loving care. His wounds were pretty bad, but it hasn't stopped him from being a wonderful husband and father," she observed.

Ruth appeared to have said all she wanted to say for the moment, and gestured with her hand for Bill to start.

Bill settled back into his chair and looked at the ceiling for several minutes, as if waiting for the stained plaster to provide him with some inspiration. Abruptly he eased himself out of his chair and walked into the bedroom. A moment later he returned carrying an old, worn, leather-bound book. For a few seconds Ruth looked surprised, but then she sighed, nodded her head, and smiled. Bill returned and repositioned a pillow before he sat down. He placed the book next to him on the armrest and spoke.

"What I have here is my father's journal. He started it when he was about ten years old, and it contains a lot of dated entries telling about events that happened in his life.

"In the back of this same book there is an attachment that mother prepared before she and my father got married. She asked father if it could be included as a part of his journal so that anyone reading it would know about Samuel and Gretchen."

Bill motioned for his children to sit on the floor in front of him. With puzzled looks on their faces, both followed their father's request.

Bill smiled at his sons, and asked them to get comfortable. They pulled a few pillows off the couch and patiently waited.

"What I want you to do is close your eyes for a few seconds before I begin the story. It will be the story that my father Samuel has written in his journal about events in his youth. It will be me telling you the stories, but I want you to visualize in your minds that the words you hear are coming not out of my mouth, but out of the mouth of my beloved father. Grandpa Samuel will be talking directly to you and will hopefully satisfy some of the questions you have about your grandparents."

Bill cleared his throat, lowered the tone of his voice slightly trying to sound as much like his father as he could.

> My name is Samuel Ezra Spader, and I was born on May 1, 1895 to Ezra Spader and Nancy Riley Spader in Pocatello, Idaho.
>
> There weren't many work opportunities for me as a ten-year-old boy. The winters were exceptionally cold in that part of Idaho and I wanted to earn money so I could purchase a coat to replace the tattered and torn sweater I routinely wore. My father would have gladly sacrificed to buy me the coat, but I knew that times were hard for dad also. I felt that I was old enough to help with the household finances, so I went about volunteering my services to anyone who might give me work.
>
> One Saturday, I saw the widow Nielsen sitting on her front porch knitting a shawl. I offered to haul and stack firewood for her. Mrs. Nielsen was elderly and frail, and didn't have anyone who could help her with odd jobs.

There was a saw mill located about a mile away from her home. I knew that the owners didn't charge people if they wanted to carry off scrap cuttings and chips. I also knew that she heated her cozy home with a small wood burning pot-bellied stove. So, I asked her if she would hire me to bring in firewood. There was only a slight hesitation before she smiled, nodded, and offered me the job. There was no mention of salary. I thanked her and then headed to a nearby granary. I found a few discarded grain sacks and after arriving at the mill, I stuffed them full with wood chips.

I carried two sacks, one on each shoulder, to balance the load. It took me the better part of the day to transport and stack the firewood and chips. I loved having a job, and I worked hard. When the work was done to Mrs. Nielsen's satisfaction, she handed me a shiny silver half-dollar coin. That was an incredible amount of money! I thanked her graciously, but before I left, she reached under the shawl on her lap and gave me something else, a book.

When she gave me this book, I opened it and was surprised to find that it contained only blank pages. There wasn't even an introduction. I first thought that she was fooling with me and I politely laughed. She also laughed and then that sweet woman smiled and patted me on my shoulder. She explained to me that it was a journal—a diary of sorts. I had never even heard that word until she gave me one. Mrs. Nielsen then patted an apple crate that sat next to her chair. I sat down and she told me that if I would write down significant events, that someday this journal would be one of my prized possessions.

Bill speaking in his normal tone added. "Boys, he took her advice to heart—sort of. He wasn't always faithful in his writing, but he did record a lot of information. The book that was once filled with nothing but blank pages now contains hundreds of pages of incredible information about the life of Samuel Spader. He told me many stories about his life over the years, but I would probably have forgotten most of them if I didn't have his journal to refer to. Remember, boys, back in those days we didn't have recording devices. Anything that was worth remembering had to be written down. Many people—like the American Indians—told stories about their lives and those of their parents, and it was then the responsibility of the children to memorize and teach their children these same stories. For instance, one of my father's first entries came on May 30, 1913. It was a Friday and father wrote the following in his journal."

> Today was a wonderful day for me. I walked through graduation ceremonies. There was a delay for a few minutes while the teachers tried to find my diploma. I am confident that most of the faculty members were also overjoyed to see me graduate. Gretchen and I spent the afternoon together. We showed off our diplomas to our parents and went for a long walk.

I can't really talk about my father's early life without including my mother. Samuel and Gretchen were both born in 1895 with only seven months separating them in age, Samuel being the older. They lived and grew up only a mile from one another, were in the same grade in school, and they were virtually inseparable.

One of the more memorable stories that Dad told me, was about my mother when she was just a little girl. I will try to share the story the same way that my father told it to me many years ago.

When Mother was about eight years old, she went with her father when he switched irrigation head gates to water our farm. She remembered standing on the bank of the canal, throwing rocks into the fast moving water. Her father shouted at her to back away from the canal, but she still had two rocks that she hadn't yet tossed. She quickly threw them into the water, but in the process she slipped on the bank and fell headfirst into the murky water. She remembered shouting for her father, but she remembered nothing else except blackness.

Benjamin, her father, later told her that he heard her scream. He raced along the bank and managed to catch a glimpse of her hair floating above the water. He sprinted to the spot and saw that she was wedged beneath the water in the crotch of a mossy tree branch. He jumped in and somehow managed to get her to the bank, but almost drowned himself in the process.

When they finally reached dry ground, Gretchen wasn't breathing. Her father frantically pushed on her back until muddy water gushed out of her mouth. He said he never quit praying, pushing, pleading, and crying the entire time. She finally rolled her eyes and coughed. Benjamin was so exhausted and relieved that he collapsed next to her and openly wept.

My mother remembered looking up into his face. His eyes were red, and he was covered with mud. He bundled her into his arms and ran to where their horse was tied, cradled mother into his arms and raced back to their house.

The doctor was summoned, and after he examined her he insisted that she stay in bed and keep warm. Even after she was up and around, she was still susceptible to most diseases. If anyone in the town caught a cold, it seemed like she would get it a day later, and it always settled in her lungs. She spent more time in bed than out, it seemed.

She was rather frail, and had trouble keeping food down or gaining weight.

Another disturbing aspect of her experience was that for a while, she was deaf. Their doctor thought that her hearing would return in time, and it did, but only in her left ear. There was only limited hearing in the right ear, and that ear problem remained the rest of her life.

Gretchen and her father were much closer after that frightening experience. It was as if a wall had been removed from between them. Her father had seldom taken time to share in the events of her life. He had always been wrapped up in caring for his animals and farm, and he seemed to care nothing about her sewing or cooking skills.

Mother was never mistreated, but after that near-drowning incident, her father made a complete reversal. From then on he took her wherever he needed to go. He became a loving escort and even attended most of her school activities and cheered her when her spirits were low.

My father told me that he was also very sensitive to my mother's hearing disability. It was awkward and sometimes embarrassing for her to have to ask people to repeat something. Some folks simply wouldn't repeat what they said, and it was like she was being rude because she couldn't hear. My father always talked to her in her good ear. Even when I was a small child before my mother died, I was conscious that she always tilted her head when I had something to say to her. I also remember that I never once remember my father ever mistreating or shouting at my mother.

Because of her hearing loss and frequent absences from school due to illness, it was difficult for her to keep up with her studies. The teachers told her parents that she would probably have to be held back a grade.

She was heartbroken and confided her plight to Samuel. He was the one person she always went to when she was depressed or exceptionally low.

When we were ready to start fifth grade, it was the decision of the teacher that they were going to keep Gretchen in the fourth grade for another year. My father had other ideas.

Bill then reached into the book sitting next to him. He retrieved an envelope from the back and took out a letter. Facing his sons, he tapped the paper and said that this was a letter that his mother had written about her fifth grade school episode. She didn't write it at the time, but she wrote it years later. He tilted back his head and held up the paper so that it was eye level. He began to read the account exactly as his mother had written it so many years ago.

To my utter surprise, on the first day of school when I sat with the other fifth grade girls, the teacher came to me, kneeled next to my desk, and whispered that I would have to repeat the fourth grade. She explained that I had simply missed too many classes because of illness. She said she was sorry, but that was the decision of the school principal.

I burst into tears and ran from the room. Samuel raced after me and as soon as we were outside I told him what the teacher had said.

Samuel told me to go back into the class and sit in that same chair along with the other fifth grade girls. I was shocked, but I did as Samuel told me.

No sooner than I got seated, Samuel picked up his chair and carried it from the boy's section and placed it right next to me so that he was near my good left ear.

He had made up his mind that he would help me through school. Rules or no rules, he was going to help me hear the teachers.

Our fifth grade teacher was livid, and she raced to Samuel and grabbed him by the nape of the neck. She tried to pull him to his feet, but he didn't budge. Samuel just sat fixed in his chair, gripping the seat with both hands. Even when she pulled his hair and tugged at his ears, the teacher couldn't budge him. She grabbed a long wooden ruler and struck him hard on his back. The other class members were caught unaware and they jumped to their feet to avoid being hit by the ruler.

Samuel didn't whimper, flinch, or even make a sound. He wouldn't even dignify her by rubbing the spots that hurt.

The teacher was red eyed and ran from the room in tears. Samuel turned and looked at me and smiled. I was horrified about what would happen next.

In a few minutes, the teacher came back with Mrs. Baker, the principal. Mrs. Baker positioned herself directly in front of Samuel. Her feet were spread, hands on her hips, and a rigid frown on her face.

Before she could utter a word, Samuel politely stood and faced her.

Mrs. Baker then shouted, "Samuel, what are you doing in the girl's section?"

He looked her square in her eyes. I will always remember his exact words.

"Mrs. Baker, I mean no disrespect, but my friend Gretchen can't hear much of what the teacher is saying. She hears very little in her right ear. I sat next to her so I could repeat in her good ear what the teacher says. If she is going to be held back a grade, then hold me back also. I will be by her side until we both graduate."

Samuel remained standing even after he was through talking. Mrs. Baker got the strangest look on her face. She politely told Samuel to sit down in his chair, the one he had placed next to me. She would discuss it with the teacher and with both of our parents.

The next day, Mrs. Baker went to my home first and complained to my father about Samuel's actions. Dad's eyes filled with tears, and a wry smile crossed his face. He looked up at the heavens and put his fingertips together under his chin.

"Thank you, dear Lord, for Samuel Spader," he said softly, almost as if in prayer.

Any dialog with the teacher was over. Visiting Samuel's parents would serve no useful purpose. She reluctantly returned to the school with her answer.

From the fifth grade right through high school, Samuel was my constant companion and tutor. He became my ears. He devoted himself to helping me get through school.

If I were ill and having difficulty reading, he would bring books to my home and read them to me.

He continued to sit in the girls' section on my left side. When I didn't hear what the teacher said, he either scribbled a note or spoke loudly enough so I would know what I had missed. He even took a "girl's home economics class," but no one of either sex ever laughed at him. Samuel had gained the respect of all the students and some of the teachers.

More than once he got in trouble with the teachers, but he made no effort to change. He was insistent that I was going to learn, regardless of how much distraction it might be to the teachers or the other students. Samuel spent more time after school cleaning blackboards and sharpening pencils than any student in the history of the school. I wanted to stay to help him, but the teachers wouldn't let me. Samuel would just smile, wave, and then dig right in and do a thorough and meticulous job. If he were told to clean two blackboards, he would do four. If a teacher wanted forty pencils sharpened, he would do eighty.

The teachers eventually realized that Samuel simply wasn't going to change, and my problem certainly wasn't going to go away. The entire teaching staff finally relented and positioned a table for Samuel and me close to the right front side of the classroom. A crude wooden partition separated us from the rest of the class while still letting me see the blackboard and the teacher.

Midway through high school, it was mutually assumed by both of us that we would someday be married and share our lives. Neither of us even considered anyone else.

Most afternoons after school, when he wasn't cleaning blackboards, Samuel would walk me home and then go directly home to work with his father on the farm. Father Ezra shared some of the farm income with Samuel, but the earnings were but a pittance. Samuel saved what money he could.

I took in laundry and cleaned people's houses. We both tried to save money, although much of my earnings went into paying for medicine and doctor's bills.

Graduation day finally came, and we were given our diplomas in alphabetical order. My last name was Morgan, so my name came before that of Samuel Spader. That didn't bother Samuel. As the names were being read,

Samuel slipped out of his place in line and walked up next to me. Some of the faculty and administrators were a little huffy and taken aback, but after a few minutes of shuffling papers, they found Samuel's diploma. My name was read, and then Samuel's. He said he was going to graduate with me, and he did it literally.

Suddenly and simultaneously, a wonderful thing happened. Every student in the building stood and loudly applauded. Most of the parents had no idea what was going on, but the students sure knew. I am confident that the majority of the faculty was overjoyed to see Samuel and me graduate, but I also know that there were several teachers who had gained a deep respect and admiration for Samuel.

Bill then added. "If you recall in Samuel's story, he talked about how wonderful it was to graduate. He also mentioned that there was some delay in finding his diploma. You can now see from my mother's letter how much of the story was missing in Father's diary entry,"

Bill put Gretchen's letter back in the envelope and inserted it into Samuel's journal.

"I have read my father's journal many, many times, especially when times were hard, or when I was lonely, or when I started feeling sorry for myself. Now I will use it to refresh my memory and keep my facts straight. Sometimes what Dad wrote in his journal was only a brief recap of events, but I do remember him telling me many details beyond what was written. My mother died when I was only four years old, so most of what happened before her death is real to me only because of the stories that my father shared about her. Father and I spent many years together, and he always loved to talk about her and keep her memory alive within me.

Bill smiled and once again lowered his voice. He reminded his boys that it was now his father's voice he was hearing.

It is Friday, May 4, 1917. Today I received a friendly greeting from President Woodrow Wilson. He has invited me to enter the service of my country. I am to report in seven days for induction into the United States Army. I informed my employer, but it came as no surprise to him. One of his sons had already received his notice. He assured me I would get my old job back when I returned and said he would pray for my safe return.

I spent most of the late afternoon with Gretchen and her parents, but she wasn't very good company since all she did was curse the Germans for making war. They had messed up our lives.

Tonight I ate dinner with my parents, but it was a rather somber gathering. Being an only son, I could possibly ask and receive a continued deferment, but I don't want that. Why should someone else have to fight in my place?

For information, the United States declared war against Germany on July 28, 1914. Many of my friends have already joined the army, but since I hadn't been called to serve, I was encouraged by family and friends to remain at home to help my father run the farm.

It is Thursday, May 10, and my induction date has arrived. Soon, an army bus will arrive at the court house in Pocatello to take me and dozens of other men to Fort Sill, Oklahoma for military training. I have been informed that I am to take along only the clothing I am wearing plus one change of underwear.

When we boarded the bus, we were issued a packet containing toothbrush, toothpaste, and a small bar of soap. It is my understanding that anything else we need will be provided after we get to Ft. Sill.

When the bus stopped for fuel, each of us inductees were allowed to stretch our legs, use the bathroom, and were provided with a sack lunch.

It is still May 11. We have been on the bus a long time and it was pitch black when we entered the gate at Fort Sill. I will write more in my journal after I find out what they are going to do with me. Our Sergeant told us that we will be given some food, but since it is almost midnight, we will probably have to eat pretty quickly. We were told the lights would be turned off after the last meal is served, and no one wanted to be last.

There is enough light coming from our bathroom that I can jot down just a few notes.

The last thirty hours have been stressful. There were sure a lot of us who showed up today. We stood in line for hours while sergeants shouted at us, sometimes for nothing at all. It is really hot and humid and I am glad I didn't bring a jacket. We all have bunk beds, and tomorrow we are supposed to be issued uniforms. We were all given fifteen minutes this evening to eat our evening meal. No time to cut up any of the food, so we just ate fast using big spoons.

Tonight I am sleeping in my street clothes.

Today is Saturday, and it is almost noon. We were harshly and unceremoniously awaked early this morning by a Sergeant grinding a coke bottle around the rim of a garbage can. It really made a terrible noise and we were all out of our cots within two minutes. I only have a few more minutes and then I am afraid that I won't be able to write much more in my journal until my training is over. The sergeant told us that we could only carry the items the army had issued, and that doesn't include my journal. They did let me keep a photo of my family, but I must mail my journal back on Monday.

It is Sunday, and I assumed that we would have the day off, but that wasn't the case. After getting up extremely early we were all issued a uniform and rifle.

I received a bolt-action Springfield. I have never fired a rifle before, but my sergeant tells me that I have to quickly learn to be proficient in its use. The uniform is extra large for me, but the supply officer said I would grow into it. It takes a while to lace up the leg wrappings.

We were all assembled just before dark for a short Sunday service. It was a multi-denominational event with representatives from various denominations each saying a few words.

Bill indicated that this was the last journal entry until after he returned home after the war. He noted that his Father did write a few notes about his training, but all of that information is contained in the brown envelope, not in the journal. Bill held up a few hand-written papers and again lowered his voice and spoke to his boys as if it were their grandfather speaking.

> I am not very sleepy, so I have decided to briefly summarize my army experiences starting with when I finished basic training.
>
> My brigade boarded a troop ship on Tuesday, July 3, 1917, in New York—destination somewhere in Europe. This was my first experience on a ship, and it was dreadful. The waves were rough, and the food was horrible. We were packed so closely to one another that we were keenly aware of our own body odor and that of our comrades. To make it worse, most of us were sick—many for the entire journey.
>
> We disembarked in England and stayed there and practiced field maneuvers for two full weeks before being loaded again onto more boats. Once in transit, we learned that our destination was France. The Germans had overrun the country, and it was our job to clear them out.
>
> After we arrived in France, most of our time was spent digging and putting wire around trenches. Shells came in continually, but the trenches gave us good cover unless it was a direct hit.
>
> One morning, we were given orders to charge forward to regain some of the ground that had been lost in a previous battle. I never even made it to the next trench. Either a bullet or a piece of shrapnel struck my left shoulder. This happened the last part of August 1917. The projectile went clean though one side and out the other. I must have really had an angel there with me because the

projectile didn't hit a bone or cut a major vein or artery. The field doctors patched me up, filled me with sulfa drugs, and let me be on light duty for four weeks.

In September, I was declared fit for duty again, and I went back to the front. It was awkward and somewhat frightening to be put in with a different group of men. In basic training, I had made some friends, but I knew nobody in the new company. I had learned to trust the man next to me, and now these men were all unknown quantities.

We were again in the trenches, and one early morning, a thick fog rolled toward us. As it got closer, those soldiers nearest the fog started to cough and gag. Our sergeant shouted for us to put on our gas masks. Most of us fumbled around with the devices, and those of us who hadn't thrown them away eventually got them on, but we were apprehensive, fearful, and slow.

I don't remember much after putting on my mask, things were pretty hectic. I woke up in a field hospital, and I stayed there until May 1918. There were many of us with the same illness. In July 1918, I was sent back to New York on a troop ship before being transferred to San Francisco. I never found out what happened to any of my first or second fighting unit comrades.

My stay in the field hospital in France and also in San Francisco was long and difficult. It is an experience that I never want to repeat.

I had a difficult time sleeping and simply couldn't find a comfortable position where I could relax. I constantly had a kerchief to my mouth and nose and simply couldn't clear my lungs of mucus. I coughed continually, and my stomach, chest, and ribs ached from the violent spasms. So many men who did get gassed eventually died of pneumonia and other complications.

I have been told that I will spend the rest of my life with lung problems because of that gas. Like all of us who serve and are injured, we pray for some miraculous cure, but the odds are against us.

Germany eventually was defeated, and everyone is declaring that this was the war that would end all wars—I sure hope so. We helped many so much, but we also lost much.

Bill then added that what he did know about his father was that it was while in combat in France, Samuel was overcome by mustard gas and had to be hospitalized. Nothing more appeared in his journal until November 17, 1918.

> This Sunday afternoon, I returned home after being gone almost eighteen months. I spent four months in the United States before being shipped to France. I was in combat for eight months and in a hospital in California for five. I was pretty much healed after two months, but the army kept me there on light duty until the war ended on November 11. It has taken me six days on trains to get home.
>
> When I got off the train in Pocatello, the platform was congested with happy banner-waving people. I was just one of several hundred neck-stretching veterans, so it took a while for me to find my family members. Gretchen was there, and after hugging our parents, I wrapped Gretchen into my arms and didn't want to let her go.
>
> We went back home and had a nice dinner. Lying next to my plate was my journal. This will be the first time I have written in it since I left Fort Sill. Mother is obviously trying to give me a hint.
>
> The back of my journal is stuffed with notes that I sent home. Maybe in a few days I will compile the information and put it in date order.

"Dad not only didn't compile the notes, he never even wrote in his journal again until just before he and Gretchen got married."

I am having a hard time going to sleep. When I finally do doze off, I wake up shouting, and my body is covered in sweat. My dreams are horrible. I know that if I sleep on my stomach or back, I end up coughing. The only sleep I get is by lying on my side—mostly my left side. I keep a window open to get a draft of air in my face. I hope to be getting married soon, but I am afraid that my sleeping habits are going to be difficult on Gretchen. Anyway, I will speak to her and see if she wants a separate bedroom.

"His next significant entry was made on Christmas Day in 1918."

Gretchen and I spent this Christmas Day with her parents. We all had a pleasant time visiting and opening our presents. Gretchen's parents gave me a hand-knitted scarf, and I gave them a handmade oak rocking chair. I made two of them and gave the other to my parents. I opened Gretchen's present. It was a heavy knitted wool sweater. It must have taken her a month to make it. I hugged her and kissed her cheek. I slipped the sweater over my head, draped the scarf around my neck. I said that I needed to try out my gifts to see if they actually kept out the cold.

I took Gretchen's coat from the rack and helped her put it on. Gently taking her hand, I led her outside. I didn't present my gift to her until we were seated on the swing in the front yard. I had to brush the snow off the seat before we could sit. It was noon, chilly, but not bitterly cold. I snuggled next to her and put my arm around her shoulder. I handed her a small box gift wrapped in white tissue paper. She smiled, sighed, and opened it.

It wasn't a big diamond, but it was all I could afford. I had worked cutting and stacking lumber for two months to save enough to buy it. Some guys buy two rings— wedding and engagement. I didn't have the money to do that. Gretchen was going to have to settle for one ring that would serve both purposes. When she opened the box, she formed an *O* with her mouth and breathed in deeply. She clutched the ring, box, and tissue to her breast. Her eyes were moist, but she didn't cry.

"Are you sure we can afford each other?" she asked.

I told her I thought we shouldn't be apart any longer. We had both been saving what money we could, but delaying our marriage longer wouldn't change things. I figured if we had both been happy and poor alone, we might as well be happy and poor together.

Gretchen nodded, and for the first time in our lives, our kiss was passionate and lasting. We had been in love since the sixth grade, but we had held ourselves for our marriage day; we still would.

I slipped the ring on her finger, and we went back into the house. Neither of us said anything about our plans. We were midway through eating our dinner before Mary noticed the ring on her daughter's finger.

She let out a shrill squeal that jolted Gretchen's father upright in his chair. Mary then pointed at Gretchen's hand. Benjamin let out a shout and jumped up and wrapped me in his arms. He told me that he wondered how long it would take us to quit saving money and start spending it.

He then let loose of me and held his daughter in his arms. He placed a gentle kiss on her forehead.

Gretchen's mother served us a piece of pie for dessert, but Gretchen couldn't swallow a bite. Mary was all smiles. Most people who knew us predicted that someday we would be married.

We went from the Morgan home to the home of my parents. We told them our plans. Their reaction was about the same as it had been at Gretchen's home. Father shook my hand and held me for a long time, occasionally patting me on my back.

"You have been a wonderful and supportive son. I only wish that I had something of value to give to you, but all I have is my love, and you have that," Father Ezra said.

Ezra then walked over to Gretchen and put his huge arm around her shoulder and pulled her close. His eyes were moist, and he had trouble getting out the words.

"I never had a daughter, and now I have the most beautiful one in the world," he told her.

Mother Nancy also held Gretchen close to her for a long time, but all those two did was cry.

We set our wedding for the first part of May 1920. Gretchen told me that she would let me know the exact date.

It wasn't until I was home and in bed that I realized that Gretchen had really never said yes, at least in words.

Today is Monday, February 3, 1919, and it has been a difficult day for me. I was sound asleep this morning when I heard a banging. It took me a moment to clear the fog from my mind before I raced to the door—it was Benjamin Morgan, Gretchen's father.

Benjamin told me that Gretchen was extremely ill, and Dr. Burgess had taken her to the hospital. She had collapsed and didn't seem to recognize anyone and didn't know where she was. She would cough, roll her eyes back, and then faint.

I put on a shirt and coveralls and put my bare feet into my boots. I didn't take time to button my shirt, put on socks, or comb my hair. I was frantic, and so was Benjamin. Benjamin had his horse, but it was only bridled. He hadn't taken the time to put on a saddle. We rode double and raced to Dr. Burgesses home. Ben held tightly to the horse's mane, and I held fast to Ben. It was bitter cold.

Dr. Burgess's home also served as the hospital, and Gretchen had been given her own room. A large white sheet formed a tent around her. A movable stove had been placed next to her bed, and the doctor was boiling water so that the steam entered the enclosure. The nurse wouldn't let either Benjamin or me into the room. It looked strange because they had packed her with ice but was blowing steam into her face.

The two of us sat in the front room of the doctor's home for four hours. At nine o'clock, Gretchen's mother came into the room. She had walked the full four miles in the snow and cold, and she looked frozen. Benjamin went to her, and they held each other for a long time. He put his coat on her and rubbed her hands and feet to get them warm.

Mary told me that she had stopped by the mill and explained to my employer why I hadn't come to work. Mary assured me that my boss said I could come back when Gretchen was feeling better.

Two hours later, the doctor came out of Gretchen's room. His head was covered with perspiration, and he looked so dreadfully tired. The white-haired man was probably seventy-five years of age, but he was still devoted to his patients.

He told us that Gretchen's fever had broken, and she was going to live. The doctor wanted her to stay at his home for a few more days so he could observe her and make sure she got needed rest. He indicated that Nurse Brandon would sleep on a cot in her room.

Gretchen's mother suggested that she stay, but Dr. Burgess waved off her offer without explanation. I think he felt that her caring for a distraught Benjamin was probably more important. The doctor made arrangements for a neighbor to drive us home in his buggy. Benjamin's horse was tied on behind.

I am not a praying man, but during the day and especially this evening, I prayed with all my being for Gretchen.

Today is Tuesday, and first thing this morning, I went to Dr. Burgess's home. It is about a three mile walk, but I ran all the way. When I got to his small hospital, Dr. Burgess was already in Gretchen's room. I could hear talking when I entered the house. One of the voices was that of my sweetheart. The doctor poked his head around the door to her room and motioned me to come in. Gretchen's parents were not there yet, but I was confident they would be shortly. It usually only took Benjamin a few moments to hitch the horse to the wagon. He had done it a thousand times, so I wasn't worried about him.

A very pale Gretchen was sitting up in bed sipping a cup of hot broth when I entered the room. The cloth drape had been removed, and she was in a fresh lemon-colored nightgown. She smiled at me as I neared her bedside. Kneeling, I placed my head on the bed near her waist. She ran her fingers through my hair and whispered comforting words to me. I tried not to show emotion, but I openly wept. She patted my shoulder and told me that she would be fine.

The doctor only let me stay a few minutes and then told me to go to work and make a living for the two of us. Apparently, he had been told of our plans.

I kissed Gretchen gently on the forehead. Her skin was warm, but not hot. I promised to see her every day.

It is Tuesday, and today Dr. Burgess let us bring Gretchen home. She has been in the hospital for nine days. Her color is slowly returning, and her raspy cough is nearly gone. The doctor wasn't able to tell us what was wrong with her, but he suggested that she was susceptible to pneumonia and to keep her warm and full of liquids.

"Gretchen did eventually recover, but she wasn't ready to go back to work until the end of March. She was fragile to start with, but at that time she only weighed eighty-five pounds."

Bill noted that his father had also mentioned in his journal that most of Gretchen's savings had been eaten up in medicine, hospital, and doctor bills. Although certainly willing, Gretchen's parents simply weren't able to help with the costs; they just didn't have any money.

"Dr. Burgess charged only a token amount for his services. He told my father that it would be payment enough if I would just take good care of sweet Gretchen. It was also in this part of his journal where my father started dating each entry." Bill observed.

> April 27, 1919 (Sunday)
> Gretchen felt good enough to attend church today, and since she wants to go—I will go. I think this is the third time I have been to church in my life, but Gretchen was rather insistent. "No one will come to our wedding if they think you are a heathen," she said.
> The preacher spoke about the need for men, women and children to write down the history of themselves as well as their parents and grandparents. Right after the meeting, Gretchen became rather insistent that I record the information while it was still fresh in my mind. The suggestion sounded like a good idea so I agreed. There was no need to argue with Gretchen, she had made up her mind.
>
> May 2, 1919 (Friday)
> Gretchen and I went for a long walk tonight after we got off work. Somehow the discussion got back to the previous Sunday sermon. Out of the clear blue, she handed me a bulky roll of paper wrapped in twine. I opened it, and to my surprise, I found that Gretchen had written down all of the information she could find or remember pertaining to her own life as well as that of her parents and grandparents.
> Gretchen told me that since we were going to be living the rest of our lives together, she thought that I should hand copy her information into my journal. She didn't seem to leave me much room for discussion or debate. I wasn't even given the option to say no! Since I would have

done anything to please her, the journal from now on will be ours, not just mine.

We walked and talked until we parted company. I am too tired to start pulling the information together tonight, but tomorrow evening after work, I will start on it. Since I have already covered much of what happened to me during my youth and my time in the military, all I have to do is some catch-up and continue to be diligent in recording what I know about my parents and grandparents, plus what new is going on in my life. When I am through, I will go into Gretchen's material and add it to my journal."

Bill then added, "They were married in a private ceremony in the Morgan home. In attendance were the minister, all four parents, Uncle James, and Aunt Lydia. Dad told me that it was the first time he had ever seen all of them together at the same time. The biggest expense of their wedding was the cost of the chicken dinner and the dollar that dad spent for the marriage license. They rented a small two-room apartment in a low-rent district west of the train tracks in Pocatello.

"Dad once told me that they were so much in love that they didn't have time to analyze how miserable their circumstances really were. They just lived one day at a time. They obviously couldn't afford to purchase a house and saw no way of ever being able to own one.

"Dad continued working with wood during the day and shoveling coal in a nearby yard in the evenings. Mom took care of other people's children. Between the two, they earned enough to neither starve nor freeze."

Glancing at his watch, Bill realized that they had been talking to Carl and Mike for several hours, and he and they needed a break.

"I think that we have been sitting here long enough for this evening, why don't we all hop in the car and go to one of those diners and let the carhops serve us an ice-cream milk shake.

When we get back, we can go on to my Grandparents story." Bill suggested.

Ruth and the other members of the family were excited about the prospect of relaxing for a while, and it would give the boy's a little while to digest what they had already heard.

Rather than have Bill walk down the hill to the car, Ruth suggested that she and the boys get the car and then pick him up.

As Ruth and the boys walked, it was Mike that was full of questions. He wanted to know why they didn't go for ice cream more often, and why didn't they ever go out to dinner together like other families did.

Ruth simply smiled at him and told him that today was just a special treat because she and their father loved them so much. For the time being, Mike seemed satisfied with the answer.

Bill was waiting at the curb outside their home when Ruth arrived. She remained in the driver's seat as Bill eased himself into the passenger seat.

"You pick the place," Bill said.

Ruth continued driving up the incline until they entered the small community of 'Hillcrest'. She drove to a nearby drive in and pulled into an empty stall. She was quickly and cordially greeted by a pretty young girl on roller-skates. The perky young girl was dressed in a bright red and white uniform and looked like a high school cheer leader. Her ponytail bobbed as the boys stared in admiration. Bill grinned but continued to look forward.

"What can I get you folks, the young lady asked?"

"How are your milk shakes? Bill asked.

Ruth and the Boys were delighted and each shouted out the flavor that they wanted.

"Four shakes then," Bill said.

It only took a few minutes before the shakes arrived

The carhop asked Ruth to roll up her window a few inches and then she attached a metal tray and pulled down a safety bracket so it would support the weight of the shakes.

Ruth gave the girl $1.50 and told her to keep the change.

This was more than just a dessert—it was an event, a mini-vacation. The family laughed and visited while they slowly finished their delicious shakes.

Ruth eventually turned on the headlights and the same smiling girl skated to the car and removed the tray.

The ride home was pleasant. Both of the boys had a lot of questions, but their mother had probably cautioned them to wait until their father was through with his story before they questioned him.

After dropping Bill off at the house, the family returned the car and returned home.

Each member of the family took their turn using the bathroom and dressing into their pajamas,

Bill again arranged his pillow in his chair and sat down. He was ready to finish with his story before bedtime.

Hating Chickens

My father, Samuel Spader, continued writing in his diary about his father (my grandfather), Ezra Samuel Spader. As Bill had done in the past, he again slightly lowered his voice so the boys could better understand that it was still their grandfather Samuel who was doing the talking.

> My parents are Ezra Spader and Nancy Riley Spader. My father was born in Seattle, Washington, on July 4, 1865. Mother was born in Pocatello, Idaho, on August 14, 1869. They were married in 1893.
>
> The two of them operated a small chicken farm on ten acres of land located about one mile south of the Seattle city limits. Their total income came from the sale of eggs and chickens. There were not wealthy by anyone's standards, but they did eke out enough money to cover their food, heat, clothing, and enough that over time they were able to purchase a small four room home.
>
> Ezra only completed six years of school before it became necessary for him to quit school and help run the farm. It took a long time, but their circumstances did eventually improve, and Ezra worked double duty so that his brother James could finish high school. James was the first member of the Spader family to have ever done so.
>
> My father and James grew up in the family home. They lived there until 1913 when their parents, Morgan and Bertha, died of smallpox within a week of one another.

Ezra was eighteen and James was sixteen at the time of their parents' deaths. The young men used most of their parents' savings to purchase a burial plot, caskets, and a headstone. The brothers had worked on the farm all of their lives, and they both hated chickens. When their parents died, the brother immediately parted company with the poultry and used the money they received from the sale to open a blacksmith shop inside the seldom-used family barn. They retained the land and raised alfalfa.

Ezra was tall, bright, handsome, and had many friends. Although uneducated, he did own half of the farm and was self-sufficient, respected, and possessed the qualities that young ladies all seemed to be searching for.

James was strong and stocky and not quite as tall as Ezra, but he also had a charming personality. Several years had passed since the death of their parents, when James began dating a beautiful girl by the name of Emma Riley. He and Emma had agreed to meet at a town dance, and she planned to bring Nancy, her younger sister. James persuaded a reluctant Ezra to come along, if nothing more than to be sociable and make Nancy feel welcome.

When the group met at the dance, introductions were made, and Ezra and Nancy naturally paired up. Ezra was bashful and not much of a dancer while Nancy was gregarious, petite, graceful, and loved to dance. She was an attractive young lady who worked as a saleslady in a ladies' clothing shop.

Ezra took a deep, nervous breath, and the two of them stepped onto the dance floor. Ezra did a lot of toe stepping, perspiring, and apologizing. After two dances, Nancy's feet were sore, and she politely suggested that they sit down and visit rather than dance. Ezra was relieved beyond measure.

They were mutually attracted to one another, and suddenly the dancing was no longer important to Nancy. She was impressed with Ezra, and it didn't matter whether he could dance or not. From that time on, the two dated.

Mostly, their activities were church socials and long walks. They occasionally attended a dance, but in consideration of Nancy's feet, Ezra danced in his stocking feet, usually away from the crowd and in the foyer, not on the dance floor. After a lengthy courtship, Ezra finally proposed marriage, and Nancy accepted. They were married a year later in 1893. I was born to this couple two years later. Dad was thirty years old when I was born, and Mom was twenty-six.

James's romantic interests in Emma didn't blossom beyond being good friends.

Nancy was willing to live anywhere just so long as she was with Ezra. Land was becoming extremely expensive in Washington State, and when they read about a six-hundred-acre parcel of land for sale in the Pocatello Valley in Idaho, they were overjoyed. They corresponded by letter with the property owner and finally reached a tentative agreement—conditional upon examination of the property. The farmland was comprised of both dry and irrigated land. The price included a farmhouse, barn, milking sheds, mature trees, a functioning sweet-water well, and many other pens and storage sheds. It was exactly what the brothers had been looking for. The total advertised price was $5,500. Ezra negotiated the price downward to $5,200.

The Seattle chicken farm was situated in a prime location, and with one hundred acres of irrigated land, a house, furnishings, barn, and farm equipment, it didn't take long to find a buyer. Most of the equipment used in the blacksmith shop was retained, but many of the very heavy items were sold. After deducting the costs associated with title transfer and banker commission, the brothers received a check in the amount of $4,300.

James spent $15 to purchase a canvas-covered sheepherders' wagon. Ezra worked over an open-bed hay wagon and attached the long tongue behind the sheep wagon. After carefully stacking, stuffing, positioning, and packing the wagons to overflowing with furniture, clothing, bedding, dishes, cookware, and tools, they made a final inspection before hitching the wagon to the four workhorses. They were ready to start their journey south to southern Idaho. The three pilgrims knelt in prayer and requested a safe journey.

Family members took turns driving on the gravel and sometimes rutted roadways. Nights were spent sleeping under the stars. The horses ate wild grass supplemented with oats and corn they brought with them or inexpensively purchased along the way. By traveling an average of thirty miles per day, they made the meandering 650-mile trip in twenty-one days, arriving in Pocatello on March 14, 1894.

Upon arriving, they had a congenial face-to-face meeting with the owner. A half day was spent examining the house, barn, and land. Then with the help of a local bank official, they closed the deal. The brothers put $4,000 down against the farm and borrowed the difference. Three hundred dollars was earmarked to partially cover their living expenses and to pay for seed and some farm equipment. They brought enough clothing, bedding, furniture, and kitchenware to sufficiently furnish the house.

Immediately upon unloading the household items, the brothers moved all of their blacksmithing tools into the barn. Within two days, they were soliciting work from neighbors to provide needed income. The covered wagon was placed behind the barn, and there it stayed.

Some of their customers paid in cash, others in food, and others bartered for the use of farm equipment. One neighbor contracted with them to repair a large steel-wheeled tractor in exchange for one workhorse and two milk cows. That was fine with the brothers because it provided them with milk, cheese, and butter.

When Ezra or James weren't plowing or planting, they would be shoeing horses or repairing saddles or farm machinery. Nancy cooked, sewed, washed, and cleaned for the two brothers. Even though both men hated chickens, they surrendered to Nancy's desire to raise some. She assured them that they would not have to do one thing with the chickens, and that one condition was sufficient for them to agree. Nancy also took over the milking and feeding chores for the two cows and the five horses.

She used one of the vacant coops and repaired all of the holes in the chicken wire. She swept, cleaned, and brought in fresh straw. Next, she made arrangements with a bachelor chicken-farming neighbor to trade fresh-baked bread, cheese, and butter in exchange for chicks and laying hens.

Within two months she had baked enough bread and churned sufficient butter and cheese to accumulate a flock of forty laying hens, sixty chicks, and one bright-eyed happy rooster.

She was selling the eggs back to her neighbor, and he was adding Nancy's eggs to his own bulk shipments. She was collecting enough money to cover all grocery and household expenses. When a hen got too old to lay eggs anymore, it became Sunday dinner.

Meanwhile, the hard work of the brothers on the farm had yielded a good crop of wheat, and they were able to buy four more workhorses. Part of their income was used to build a large milk shed, and they purchase fifteen more milk cows. Nancy was mercifully relieved of her milking and livestock feeding responsibility for which she was exceedingly happy. With the addition of the extra cows, their days became even longer, but the dairy business was also yielding a good profit. By the end of their first year, they had built a milk shed and cooler and decreased their bank obligation down to $500. Life was good.

In June 1895, James met a charming young lady at a church social. They were immediately attracted to one another, and he and Lydia Wilson were married five months later. Naturally, Ezra was the best man.

Lydia was a tall handsome woman. She was stately and athletic. She and Nancy became the best of friends, and it was like they had always known and loved one another.

Ezra and Nancy used one of the bedrooms, and James and his bride used the guest room on the other side of the house. The arrangement worked fine until late 1895 when I was born. The four adults then mutually agreed that there needed to be a change in the living arrangements.

A tree-shrouded plot of ground was selected nearby, and the brothers immediately dug a well and began to build a house for James and Lydia. Most of the brothers' savings was used to cover the cost of lumber, glass, and furnishings.

The house wasn't as large as Ezra's farmhouse, but it was new, clean, comfortable, and suited James and Lydia just fine.

Of course, I don't remember any of this, but that is what I was told by my parents.

In 1898, a severe drought hit the area, and the canal serving the farm dried up. With most of the sugar beets under irrigation, it only took a couple of months for the crop to wither and die. Far worse, there was an invasion of grasshoppers. Most every leaf, blade, and twig still standing was consumed by the hoppers. Within the year, the Spader family savings were depleted, and the brothers were forced to go back to the bank with hat in hand. When the two men left the bank, they were now in debt $2000—$900 more than when they first bought the farm.

The farm could no longer support two families, so James and Lydia moved to Pocatello, some ten miles away. He and his wife rented a hovel home. James leased some inexpensive space and opened a blacksmith shop within walking distance of their shack. Since the brothers brought most of their tools with them from Seattle, there wasn't much of an investment required for James to get started.

Within a year, James had earned enough to make a down payment on a home.

Unfortunately for Ezra and Nancy, conditions on the farm weren't getting better. There was still only limited water, and all of the land had to be dry-farmed. The income dropped to less than 20 percent of what it had been just two years earlier. Luckily the wells hadn't dried up, so there was ample water for the milk cows. Stored hay, bran, and wheat would take care of the cows, chickens, and other farm animals. Neighbors continued to buy eggs, milk, cheese, and butter, but that income was insufficient to maintain the farm.

Even by working sixteen hours a day, Ezra wasn't able to generate enough income to make much progress on paying the bank. Since both men still owned the farm jointly, they made the decision to again solicit cooperation from the bank. They needed more money, but they also wanted to extend the payment provisions of their existing loan.

The bank was having its own problems, and not only wouldn't the bankers advance more money, the brothers were immediately served with a notice. If the note wasn't paid in full within ninety days, the bank threatened to repossess the farmhouses, land, and other assets. The brothers left the bank very depressed.

In September 1899, the bank was finally forced to foreclose—520 acres were sold to cover the bank note. The farm shrunk down to eighty acres of irrigated land, but they were able to retain the houses and the chicken and milk businesses.

The two men had always been close, and James unselfishly deeded his share of the remaining property to Ezra.

Ezra continued to operate the farm the best he could, but even more depressed conditions drove down the price of wheat. Six months later, Ezra and Nancy lost everything but their clothing, furniture, and personal effects.

The property was sold at auction, and the new owner immediately moved his family into the farmhouse and his parents into James's house. He was sensitive to Ezra's plight and offered him a job and let him use a large shed that was once used to store wheat and bran.

Nancy somehow kept her good attitude. Some whitewash on the outside walls, curtains over the windows, and within two weeks, she had the shack looking like a home. It was tough on Ezra to share crop on the same land that he had purchased and developed.

"You will hear more about those days as we finish reading my grandfather's journal. Once when I was about ten years of age, my dad told me, 'My parents [Ezra and Nancy] were very poor and always owed more than they earned. I have been able to carry on that family tradition with dedication and great success.'

"Come to think about it, I have been able to carry on that same family trait pretty well myself. I hope that you boys can break that string," Bill added.

Sheep, Turkeys, and Tutors

"If you recall, Mother Gretchen gave Samuel a bundle of notes and records of her family's history. Samuel was planning to include the information in his journal, but he ultimately gave up primarily because it was just too long. Instead, he created a packet attachment and put it in the back of the book. What I will read is what Gretchen had to say about her own life, and then how her life was intertwined with that of Samuel."

My name is Gretchen Stoll Morgan. I was born on July 14, 1895, in Pocatello, Idaho. I was the first of two children born to Benjamin and Mary Stoll Morgan. My brother Benjamin died when he was just three years old.

My parents were also born in Pocatello—Dad in 1860 and Mother ten years later.

My father had very little education, but through some type of "divine intervention," he got involved with the sheep business. Eventually, my father and mother cared for hundreds of sheep. Most people called them sheepherders, but my father preferred to be called a shepherd, like in biblical times.

He wasn't much of a penman, so my mother assembled Benjamin's notes and wrote down the following information about my father.

Benjamin (Ben) completed six years of school. His father, Benjamin Sr., was seriously injured in a farm accident and lost the use of his left hand. Ben, being the eldest son, had to quit school to help support his family by taking over the responsibilities of the farm. Ben could still do many things, but he was limited in his ability to perform manual labor. Through the years, Ben hefted many bales, and working with a pick and shovel, he dug wells, canals, ditches, and furrows. His hard work paid off in the form of powerful arms and torso.

Ben just figured that hard farmwork was his lot in life and had pretty much resigned himself to that end. Then when he turned eighteen, his luck changed for the better. A Spaniard by the name of Jon Caspoli moved into Pocatello Valley and leased thousands of acres of mountain property from the state of Idaho—and he began raising sheep.

Jon couldn't do the work alone and was in need of help. He approached Ben with an offer. Jon's English was very limited, but through a Mexican interpreter, he was able to convince Ben to work for him. The pay was a pittance, but when he offered a percentage of both the profits and the flock, Ben's interest was piqued. He talked the proposal over with his father and mother, and because Ben's two younger brothers were fully capable of assuming the farm responsibilities, Benjamin Sr. was eager to see his eldest son improve his circumstances. A local banker fashioned a contract, and with the stroke of a pen, Ben was suddenly a businessman.

Ben's board and room were provided. The herder's food was mostly beans, hardtack, wheat bread, coffee, venison, and mutton and his shelter was in a canvas-covered sheep wagon, but Ben was content.

For the next fourteen years, he worked and lived with sheep. At shearing time, he received his percentage of the profits, and when the lambs or sheep were sold, he was rewarded with his fair share of the income.

When the sheep were moved or sold in the winter, Ben moved back to the farm to help with construction, repair, and fix-up jobs. He knew that he would never be wealthy, but his bank account was growing.

Then one fateful day, the state of Idaho passed a law prohibiting further grazing of cattle and sheep on the same certain sections of public forestland. Notice was given to Jon that his lease would be terminated in two years. Jon made the decision to sell his half of the sheep to Ben, move to Wyoming, and retire next to a trout stream. At that time my father was thirty-three years old.

Over the years, Ben had accumulated a stockpile of over $4,000. He figured that if he had another $2,000, he would have enough to purchase some mountain grazing land and could replenish his own flock.

He searched and finally found a rancher in Kemmerer, Wyoming, who was willing to sell him one thousand acres of land for $5,000, but Ben needed another thousand. He put down a $3,000 deposit and agreed to pay the other $2,000 in one year. The contract was drawn up and signed.

Jon was aware of Ben's need to raise more money, so he came to the rescue. He offered to continue working with the sheep until the forest service lease ended. Ben was ecstatic and thanked Jon profusely. They entered a verbal agreement that the two men would fairly divide the profits. A handshake was all that was required to seal the deal. Ben left his remaining money in the bank and immediately started looking for work. He had two years to come up with the additional funds, and he wasn't about to lose his deposit.

Still as strong as a bull, he knew he could handle most any job, but only as a last resort would he go back to working with a pick and shovel.

A shipping company in Pocatello was in the process of unloading a backlog of massive amounts of freight from hundreds of railcars. Ben joined several unemployed men waiting on the loading dock. All of them needed and were hoping for temporary or permanent work. The hiring boss emerged from his office after calculating his additional manpower requirements. "I need two men!" he shouted.

He held up two yellow cards and happened to be right next to Ben when he made his announcement. Within seconds, Ben gingerly snatched one of the cards. The foreman didn't object. There was a stir of activity and murmuring in the background, but that was of no concern to Ben—he had the pass and the job.

Ben worked eighty-four hours per week for three weeks to unload the cargo. When the work ended, the foreman handed Ben a chit that detailed the pay rate and number of hours he had worked. Ben was sent to the payroll office.

The secretary was a lovely young lady by the name of Mary Stoll, and Ben was smitten with her beauty and lovely smile.

While the paymaster was calculating Ben's pay, Ben simply couldn't quit looking at her. Their eyes kept meeting, and each time he got caught, he would blush. He was a rather bashful fellow, but she captivated him.

It took a lot of courage, but that afternoon, Ben waited outside the office until quitting time. Mary emerged, and Ben tipped his hat, reintroduced himself, and timidly asked her if he might walk her home. She was reluctant, but since it wasn't far and the sun was still out, she agreed.

The short trip ended up taking over two hours. The two shared stories and talked about their lives. Ben learned that Mary's parents had both died of cholera when Mary was but two years of age. Mary's mother had a sister who was a spinster schoolteacher, and it was she who raised Mary. Mary benefited from an abundance of love, and she received a good education. Her aunt died when Mary was seventeen—in Mary's last year of high school. She inherited her aunt's small house located next to the school and had been on her own ever since. She was beautiful, multitalented, independent, and intelligent.

A good-night kiss was not even entertained, but their gentle handshake was long and tender.

Either Mary had influence in the hiring process or else Ben was an exceptionally good worker, because for whatever reason, he kept getting jobs at the dock.

The cash in the bank coupled with the dock income was sufficient for Ben to contemplate marriage. He and Mary had been dating for well over a year, and one moonlit evening in front of her home, Benjamin handed Mary a bouquet of roses, knelt in front of her, and proposed. She happily and tearfully accepted.

Mary and Ben were married on September 1, 1894, and I was born one year later.

Jon Caspolli stood in as best man and was as proud as a peacock. His wedding gift to the couple was three hundred dollars plus all of the wagons, horses, sheepdogs, and equipment at such time as the flocks were sold. Ben was overwhelmed. Jon had made the decision that once his shares of the sheep were sold, he would use his share of the income to retire.

The young married couple spent three delightful days together before it was time for Ben to start buying lambs and planning the move of his flock to their new grazing area. Jon helped in the buying process, and one week later he helped Ben and three other workers to move Ben's share of the flock to Wyoming.

A qualified driver navigated the lead wagon, Mary drove the second, and Jon followed behind on horseback. Ben directed the work efforts of the other herders and the sheepdogs.

The property was located about 150 miles from Pocatello, but the trip was over level ground, and it took only sixteen days to move eight hundred sheep and lambs.

It was a beautiful evening when they arrived in Kemmerer, and after the laborers had been paid, Ben, Mary Stoll, and Jon sat around the campfire reminiscing. Over the years Ben had acquired some Spanish and Jon had learned to speak broken English, but neither man was proficient in the other's language.

Jon was a soft-spoken man and had never been talkative, but this night he had something he wanted to say. He looked directly at Ben and spoke.

"I never married, and you closest thing to me having son. I love you as my own. I wish you both long lives and many children, and may children be honorable like papa." Jon then swept his hat across his waist and bowed.

Ben rose and went to his friend. The two men embraced each other for a long time. Jon bowed once more, tipped his hat, and mounted his horse. Mary encouraged him to spend the evening and leave in the morning, but he had made up his mind. He was off to Pocatello to sell his sheep and start a new life.

"I love mountains and smell of forest. I know stars and will travel with full moon. I have bedroll and hardtack, what more I ask? I am leaving only true friends I have. I pray to Almighty that we meet again before my bones turn to dust. Adios, amigo."

Ben feared that he would probably never see his old friend again. The tears welled up in his eyes.

Ben held the two young collie dogs while their mother followed at the heels of Jon's horse. The dogs whined and jerked to get free so they could follow, but Ben held them fast.

Jon swiveled in his saddle and shouted back, 'Tie them until morning then they no follow! Once out of sight, they calm down. Sprinkle pepper behind horse tracks. One sniff, they forget Mama.'

And he was right—the dogs whined most of the evening, but before sunrise, everything was quiet. The sheep were still, and the air was fresh and cool. The next morning, Ben reluctantly and hesitantly turned the dogs loose. They sniffed for a few minutes, snorted, shook their heads, and then settled into their routine of rounding up the wandering sheep—they would stay.

My parents worked with sheep until 1897, when Mother was delighted to learn she was pregnant. It was difficult for Mary with one small child in the mountains, but she never complained.

Then one day Father made the decision to give up his sheep and spend the rest of his life with his family in a house—not in a wagon.

Within a month, he had contracted to sell the land, sheep, and all of his equipment to a rancher from Jackson. Ben's bank account was nearly $9,000, a fortune in those days. My parents had great plans.

My father had a real gift with animals. He moved his family back to Pocatello and purchased eighty acres of land, built a barn, a dozen sheds, and started raising turkeys. Mother kept the books.

After building a house and work shed, purchasing turkeys, and paying for the land, he and Mother still had over $1,000 in their bank account. They weren't worried because there was a good market for turkeys, and when the fattened birds were sold in October, they would have plenty of money.

That day never came. In late September, when I was about three years old, a severe thunderstorm hit, and for several hours the lightning flashed and the rain and thunder blasted our farm. We were in the house safe, but the turkeys didn't fare as well.

A turkey is an unusually stupid bird. When they get frightened, they panic and tend to huddle tightly together. Dad had a huge shed with several individual compartments to house the birds, so there was plenty of room and protection. He had checked on them before going to bed, and everything seemed to be fine, but sometime during the evening, when the thunder got loud, the birds apparently panicked.

Early the next morning when Ben went out to do his morning chores, he was overwhelmed and devastated to discover that over 70 percent of his birds were dead. The frightened birds had huddled together in one of the compartments so compactly that most of them died of suffocation. He was heartbroken, and most of their investment was gone in one night.

The remaining turkeys were sold at auction two weeks later, but the gain from the sale was barely enough to cover the costs of transporting the birds. He wanted to start over, but the money he had wasn't sufficient. He met with bankers, but they considered turkey farming a risky investment—his loan request was denied.

He still had his home and barn, so with some of the money he purchased a dozen milk cows and made ends meet by selling milk, butter, and cheese. Mary cared for my baby brother and me and did the best she could with limited resources. How quickly life can take a turn.

I grew up less than a mile from where Samuel Spader was born.

Samuel was my closest and dearest friend, and I have loved him since I was just a child. There was never a doubt in my mind that someday we would be married. Samuel may have had some uncertainty, but I will take care of that concern.

We met in grade school and frequently played together during the early evenings and on weekends. I don't believe that either of us ever courted anyone else; I know I didn't.

Our families were certainly not part of any social circle. They supported us, and we were never cold or hungry, but we were isolated from those who had money. Samuel lived in a little house with his father.

Wherever we went, we either rode a horse or walked. Neither of our parents ever owned an automobile.

I was older than my baby brother, Benjamin Jr. He was born in Pocatello in 1897. He was only three when he was killed in a freak accident on New Year's Day in 1900. That was just shortly before my father had lost his turkey business.

Apparently, people were celebrating the new millennium, and several of the younger kids were crawling around the barn on snow-covered bales of straw. Ben and I were both playing together on the dirt floor, and the vibration must have loosened one of the bales, and it tipped from the loft and landed on top of Ben's head. It broke his neck, and he died instantly. My memory of the event is what I have been told.

My parents were devastated. Ben was such a happy and gentle child, and his absence impacted the family greatly. I often wondered what my life would have been like had he lived. I wasn't old enough to realize that he was gone, but even now, I am aware of how many tears were shed by my parents. His birthday would roll around, and they would cry. They would shed tears at the mention of their only son's name.

He is buried in a small cemetery not far from here.

Welcome to Logo

Bill opened the book and skipped over several pages before he found what he was looking for.

"I will read from the information my father has written. If you recall, he got this book when he was only ten years old. He wrote a few things in his early years, but it was obvious that he wasn't much interested in maintaining a daily diary. He mentioned about killing a blackbird with a slingshot and wrote about a time when he got measles and almost died. He also showed deep remorse when he stole a watermelon from a neighbor's garden, but these are not the major elements of his life. What I am going to read in length is his story about how he got a job with the Union Pacific Railroad."

Bill cleared his throat, adjusted his glasses, squinted a few times, and then started to read.

> May 4, 1921 (Wednesday)
> Gretchen and I have been married a little over a year now. Recently, a friend of mine told me about a contract that Union Pacific Railroad has been awarded. It is a five-year effort to build a rail line from Pocatello, Idaho, to Salt Lake City, Utah.
> At the employment office this morning, I filled out a work application. The posting will not be announced for two more days, but the UP official was kind enough to let me to fill out the employment application.

May 6, 1921 (Friday)

For the past two days, I have checked in with UP before going to work, and then again as soon as my shift was over. Today was my lucky day. I was at the UP station before the employment doors opened. The bulletin was posted as soon as the office opened, but I didn't need to even look at it. While the long line of applicants were reading the notification and filling out job forms, I was already interviewing with a Union Pacific official.

I didn't need to know if the job would have any paid time off for vacation or sick time, but what I did know was that it offered fair pay and guaranteed work for five years. The fact that it also provided living accommodations and a family food allowance was a luxury. Those things alone made it enticing for Gretchen and me, but it was the potential of working for my own land that is going to be the biggest prize. Successful applicants were to be given the option of working with full pay or working for half pay and receiving a "land credit." I desired the security and stability that accompanies land ownership. When the interviewer had completed reviewing my application, he advised me that by signing the paper, I would be obligating myself to work six days a week for the full five years. I nodded my head in approval. Having already selected the half-pay land option, the interviewer asked me whether I preferred 160 acres of dry farm or eighty acres of irrigated. Without hesitation, I told the man I wanted the irrigated land, and he checked the appropriate box.

The interviewer explained that an agreement had been reached between UP and the US government. The government handled the paperwork relating to land acquisitions, trades, and leases and had already acquired the land and deeded it to UP. The land could be sold, traded, or used as an incentive to workers, just so long as the government benefited through cost reductions and an on-time completion schedule.

The land adjacent to the railroad was retained for use by UP for further expansion. The peripheral land was earmarked for the "land credit" workers.

I was shown a map of available sites and chose one in southern Idaho about twenty miles from the Utah border. There was ample water. The land parcel I chose was out of a flood plain but was only one-half mile from a large river. I knew from the contour map that additional water could be pumped or channeled to where my farm was located. The description captivated my interest when it described the parcel as being sandy loam soil located in a valley surrounded by mountains.

Father Ezra told me many times, "The good Lord only made so much land, there won't be any more. You own a piece of this good earth, and you won't be beholden to anyone."

The interviewer signed the document and then handed me a pen, and I signed and dated it. A clerk then notarized our signatures.

I asked the official when I would know if my application had been accepted. He smiled and told me that he was the person who made the employment decision.

"Mr. Spader, for the past two minutes you have been an employee of the greatest railroad company in the world, Union Pacific."

I couldn't contain my emotions, and I laughed and cried at the same time. We shook hands, and as I was leaving, he put his hand on my shoulder and handed me a small booklet that outlined what was expected of UP employees. The document explained about Union Pacific's rules regarding personal hygiene, tardiness, attitude, and various other company rules and regulations.

The clerk handed me a carbon copy of the contract and informed me that I had been the very first person to sign up for the program.

Bill interjected, "My dad told me that the land-credit-option strategy worked out well. About a quarter of the five-year contract workers elected the half-pay option."

He found his place on the page and started reading again.

I walked out of the building and sat on the steps while I read the document from cover to cover. Gretchen and I were not going to starve, and if we were frugal with our money, we could probably build up a nest egg. I read about the pay rate and happily realized that one-half of my new salary from UP would be twice as much as I was currently making working in the coal yard.

I reread the contract that outlined all of UP's guarantees and memorized the description of the property and the surroundings. I am even going to be given title to my own water shares. My heart is very full, and I feel blessed beyond words.

Before going to my job at the lumber mill, I stopped at the bank and closed out our savings account and put $220 in my pocket.

Reporting for work, I told my boss that today would be my last day, that I had accepted a job with UP. My boss was cordial and said he would miss me. He looked at the railroad job as being secure and stable. He wished me good luck, and we shook hands. I wanted to skip the coal yard work and race home to Gretchen, but I knew it wouldn't be right. It was a long shift, but I felt an obligation to finish the day. I worked harder than I ever had. I shoveled coal, smiled, and shoveled some more. At the end of my shift, my boss handed me an envelope with my pay. He included an extra twenty dollars. I was very touched.

Stuffing the money into my pocket, I ran all the way home. My pocket was bulging with bills.

When I walked into the room, Gretchen sensed that something was different. I gently pushed her into a chair and let her know how I had been spending my day. She couldn't stay seated. She jumped up and down and threw her arms around my neck. She simply couldn't speak. All she did was cry with joy and squeeze me even tighter. This was the first time in my life that I felt that I could see light at the end of the tunnel.

A note attached to my contract indicated that my family and I should be on the front steps of the Pocatello courthouse at six o'clock Friday morning. We went to bed, but neither of us did much sleeping. We were too busy digesting what had happened today.

May 12, 1921 (Thursday)
I had been told by UP that all I should bring with me was clothing and personal necessities. Whatever else we needed would be provided once we got to Logo, Utah.

I spent the day visiting with neighbors, encouraging them to purchase our furniture. It took me six visits, but by seven o'clock this evening, I had sold and delivered most household items. I got thirty-five dollars for our bed, dresser, one chair, bedding, and towels, and another forty-five dollars came from the sale of our remaining chairs, couch, dishes, and washtubs. I had to borrow a horse and wagon to deliver the furniture I had sold. When I was finished, I returned the wagon, unhitched the horse, and put it back into its stall.

We packed all of our clothing and personal items into one large suitcase. Our spare food fit into a wicker picnic basket.

Bill interjected, "Gretchen was very tired after the long day, and after she went to sleep, Samuel recapped the events of the entire day. This particular section of his journal is one of the longest and most detailed of anything he wrote."

May 13, 1921 (Friday)
This has been a long but eventful day. Last night, we spread pine boughs on the floor and covered them with a

blanket. I slept better than I had expected, except for being awakened a few times by the sound of Gretchen's giggles.

We got up early, washed in the sink, and dressed. Gretchen used one of the pine boughs to sweep out the needles and get the "shack" in presentable condition.

As instructed, Gretchen and I were on the courthouse steps at six. She gave me six dollars and seventy-five cents. She wanted me to tie the coins in the corner of my handkerchief, but I absolutely refused. She had sewn the rest of our money, over three-hundred dollars into the hem of her slip.

A short time later, a four-passenger buggy arrived. Our luggage was loaded on top and strapped into place. We were on our way.

Our destination was Logo, Utah, a place we had never even heard of and weren't able to locate on our map. Two railroad executives rode with us. The conversation was strained for a while, but eventually they became more sociable. We were both commended for our decision to take the "land credit" option.

It was a long, hot, hard ride. The driver stopped at a small town midway between Pocatello and Ogden, Utah, to give the horses water and grain. While we were stopped, the two executives went to a local diner and got something to eat. Gretchen retrieved some peanut butter and jelly sandwiches from the basket. After eating, we spent a few minutes walking off some of our aches and pains, but never strayed far from the buggy.

It had been seven hours since we left Pocatello, and we were overjoyed when we finally arrived at the railway station in Ogden.

Ogden was a central hub for Union Pacific, and there were lines going in every direction. The driver provided us with passes and told us where to board the train headed for Reno, Nevada. Gretchen looked alarmed, and the driver sensed her concern.

"You won't be going to Reno, ma'am. Only as far as Logo," he smugly informed her.

There was a wait of two hours before the train left, but it gave us time to get the dust out of our lungs and breathe in some fresh air. Sure enough, the boarding platform was right where the driver told us it would be. We boarded, and for the first time in our lives, we were going to ride a train. What a marvelous adventure. Neither of us had been more than thirty miles from Pocatello. Now we were off on a journey of over two hundred miles. The ride from Ogden to Logo took another hour, and it was certainly more comfortable than the buggy had been. We were both full of awe and were amazed at the speed the train traveled through the beautiful countryside.

When the conductor announced that we had arrived at Logo, Gretchen breathed a sigh of relief.

We stepped into a lush green valley surrounded by forested mountains. It was a beautiful place. UP probably never put a railway station in a nicer location, I thought. The porter helped me with the suitcase while Gretchen held tight to the picnic basket.

The town, if you could call it that, was an assortment of large and small buildings. An immense round building with four large double doors dwarfed all of the other structures. We were excited to learn more about Logo, but not right now. It had been eleven hours since we left Pocatello, and we were ready to take a bath and relax in our new living quarters. Gretchen was looking a little pale. This had almost been too much for her.

We followed the other departing passengers on a wooden platform that led around to the front of the building. The station housed the town's only store, and attached to it was an elevated wheel-less UP dining car that had been converted into an eatery.

I carried the suitcase. Gretchen still tightly clutched the picnic basket in both arms. She must have thought there were a lot of basket bandits lurking in Logo.

Outside the entrance to the store, I sat the suitcase on a wooden luggage rack. Gretchen reluctantly attached the basket to the case with one of the suitcase's long leather straps.

"By the way, the basket that we take to the beach is the same one that belonged to my parents," Bill noted.

We had expected to see only magazines, newspapers, candy, and tobacco, like had been the case in Ogden, but we were delighted to see shelves stocked with a variety of foodstuff and clothing. This was a regular "big city" store.

The dining car was attached to the store by way of a covered walkway. The passageway between the store and the diner assured that no one would enter the diner without first weaving through the store merchandise.

I saw a man dressed in a green apron, and after the gaggle of passengers had departed into the diner, I approached him.

I explained that I had recently been hired by the railroad and needed to speak to someone about our living accommodations.

"Oh, you must be the Spader family. I am Seth Brown. I am so happy to make your acquaintance." He vigorously shook my hand and bowed to Gretchen. "My wife and our two sons run the store and diner. Anyway, on behalf of Union Pacific and us, we want to welcome you both to Logo."

Mr. Brown whispered something to a woman behind a counter. He pointed politely to us, and she smiled and waved. He removed his apron, draped it over the back of a chair, and led us out of the store into the sunlight. I picked up the suitcase, and Mr. Brown grasped the picnic basket. It took us a moment to unwind the leather strap. We all walked and visited as we proceeded toward a line of cabooses.

As we left the store, he pointed next door to a three-story building.

"That is a new structure, only been here two years. It was built to house the train engineers and other professional railroad workers. There are twelve engineers and their families who live here year round. Their regular job is to drive passenger and freight engines. Union Pacific sets up the schedule so that there are always at least three engines here. If helper engines are needed, then these men are available. I will tell you more about that later.

"This building also houses one large room that serves as the school for children up through the sixth grade. Mrs. Harwood is a certified teacher, and since she happens to be married to one of the engineers, it made for a good working situation. UP hired her and provides all of the classroom materials. The older children, after they are twelve years old, leave Logo and attend school in Ogden. UP is pretty good with those students also. The company renovated and customized one of the retired dining cars into a classroom. It is only hooked to a train on weekdays and is for the exclusive use of students from Logo. The car is equipped with tables, soft chairs, lots of books, and paper. A student, if so inclined, can study to and from school in a lighted, warm, and comfortable atmosphere. The train stops near the junior high and the high school. Pretty smart bunch of kids come from here. Mrs. Harwood does a good job of preparing them. Last year, the Ogden High School student body president was from Logo.

"If you folks are churchgoers, we use the same room for church services as the kids do for school. We don't mind mixing church and state here. Services start at nine in the morning. We don't have a paid minister, so we come and worship in our own way. Occasionally, we have someone who is passing through who will stop and give us a real bang-up sermon. I will serve as church coordinator, if you will, and get the meeting started. We don't have a piano or organ, so you need to spruce up on you're a cappella voice."

We continued our tour of the town. As we passed the large round building, I asked Mr. Brown what it was.

"That's the roundhouse," he said.

I snickered and told him that the name certainly fit. Mr. Brown then recited a brief history of Logo and why the town was created.

Bill commented that Mr. Brown provided a lot of information and quoted him quite often throughout his journal.

"A locomotive can be driven inside the building and rotated on the movable turntable. It can be repaired, refurbished, and then headed out in the direction it will next be needed. All spare parts, tools, and equipment required to maintain an engine are stored inside the building. The mountains surrounding Logo are quite tall, and if the trains are pulling a lot of cars or if the weather is bad, even with the use of wheel sand, the locomotives can't make the climb up the steep grades without help. The other three big structures adjacent to the roundhouse contain helper engines. There are six of them, two in each building. Those engines are high-powered steam engines that can push or pull a train over the mountains. The dispatchers have a pretty good idea of when they will be needed, so at least one of them is always kept running. A helper takes a while to warm up, and UP can't chance having a train stranded in those mountains. A stalled train can impact the whole operating schedule for the entire western United States. Ten years ago, all six helpers were out at the same time. It was a memorable sight. The snow was five feet deep, and it took three helpers per train to get them over the pass. No one was idle in Logo that particular evening. When a helper engine is needed, it is driven into the roundhouse and swiveled until it is pointed in the direction it needs to go. When it returns, it is returned to one of the three sheds. Each helper has its private storage stall—like a prize racehorse.

"Farther down the road, you can see that long building with a lot of windows. That is where the railroad transient work crews live. Those guys are a tough and sometimes mean lot. There is a conglomerate mix of nationalities and races housed in that building. Most of the workers are Orientals, but UP also hires a lot of Mexicans, Negroes, Whites, and some Indians. Some of the men stay here for several months, others for just a few days. They go where UP needs them. A few of them are married, but none of them are allowed to bring their wives here. When the men get vacation time, most of them leave Logo for a while. Others have no place to go, so they just stay here until they are reassigned to another station. Union Pacific intentionally built that structure so it would be as far away from the engineers' apartments as possible. The transients are rather clannish and sometimes make a lot of noise. On occasion they get drunk, rowdy, fight, and do things that irritate the rather temperamental engineers. We leave the transients alone, and they seldom bother us. Many of them work seven days a week wherever UP needs them. Most of the engineers and their wives won't even talk to the transients," Mr. Brown said.

We passed dozens of other small sheds and storage barns, but Mr. Brown didn't consider them important to the tour. As we approached a line of cabooses, the storekeeper must have seen some doubts in our faces.

"Don't let the outside appearance fool you. These units have been modernized and converted into very comfortable living quarters. The units stay cool in the summer and warm in the winter because of the excellent insulation. The engineers and their families lived here until two years ago when UP built the apartments. These cabooses have all the amenities you will need. There are twelve of them, and they are identically furnished except for the color of the curtains and rugs," Mr. Brown said.

He opened the door, and we stepped inside. There was a sink and a door leading to an inside toilet and tub, the first we ever had. There were cupboards stocked with dishes, pots, pans, closets, pull-down ironing board, desk, four chairs, and a table. Separate doors led into the small bedrooms at the rear of the unit. Further inspection revealed a dresser, full-length mirror, and more closets. The unit had curtains, blinds, and front and back porches.

Mr. Brown continued, "UP plumbed the units so that you have inside running water. UP workmen buried the waterline six-foot underground, and it has never frozen up since it was installed. I doubt it will freeze up anytime in the future.

"I don't know exactly where you will be working, Samuel, or what you will be doing, but I am confident that you will be home in the evenings. UP has widely publicized the 'land credit' program, and they anticipate getting good public relations mileage. If a reporter ever asks you what you think of the program, I suggest you give it some serious thought before you answer. Negative publicity isn't good for railroad employee tenure.

"You can get your wood and coal from the bins in back of your units. Transients stock the bins except for kindling. You can collect bits of scrap wood from the loading dock where they bust open the wooden crates.

"Come to the store at seven o'clock on Monday morning to get a mailbox and sign some other paperwork. You should be ready to board the work train promptly at eight. You needn't bring a lunch, but you do need a good pair of work gloves. I can give you credit for a pair if you don't own any. You can pay me when you get your first check.

"The other families will be in later this evening or by noon tomorrow. Since you two are now familiar with the units, would you mind welcoming the new families and helping them get settled?" he asked.

I assured him we would be happy to do that.

He further suggested that I put families with children together down at the far end of the line.

"It will allow the mothers a better opportunity to watch the children while the youngsters are playing outside," Mr. Brown observed.

I nodded my concurrence, thanked him, and shook his hand. Mr. Brown, while still holding my hand, told me to call him Seth.

"We are going to be around each other for five years, so let's not be so gall-darned formal. I'm an employee of UP just like you folks."

Inside our unit, I wrapped Gretchen into my arms and kissed her gently. I told her that I loved her and reassured her that she would be happy here.

"This home is nicer than any place I have ever lived, and we don't have to pay rent." She giggled.

While still holding her tightly, I casually suggested that maybe it was time for us to think about starting our own family. My comment brought out all of Gretchen's pent-up emotions, and she burst into tears. It wasn't one of those mild cries, but an outward, bellowing, full-blast explosion. My shoulder was wet. I guessed that her answer must mean yes.

In that instant, we both knew the quality of our lives would improve.

I placed the suitcase on the kitchen table, and Gretchen, through bleary eyes, unpacked our earthly possessions, which weren't all that many. She hung up the few articles of clothing in a closet and put our toothbrushes, combs, towels, and washcloths in the bathroom. She tucked our nightwear under the pillow on the bed, and with the exception of my journal and a couple of books, we were unpacked. I stowed the few apples and pears left in our picnic basket in the pantry. It took us all of five minutes, and we were moved in.

The location was perfect. It was close to where we workers would board the train. It was ideal for the women because they could raise a garden, and the soil was fertile. The scenery was magnificent. From our back porch, we could see a waterfall flowing down the snowcapped forested mountains. All around us were pine trees, squirrels, chipmunks, deer, and rabbits. A crystal clear stream ran within two hundred feet of our backyard. Oh, we were in heaven at last. I might even take up trout fishing!

Our living quarters were close to the store, and to Gretchen's relief, the store carries most of the food items we will need. She has never had access to a stove where she could make bread. She is going to buy some flour with our first paycheck and learn how to bake.

"Oh my, oh my," she said to me.

Knowing we wouldn't be able to sleep, we elected to walk off our nervous energy and familiarize ourselves with our new surroundings.

An area had been roped-off for use by the tenants where we could have our own gardens. Several water pumps were strategically place that would provide the necessary water.

Seth had told us about the roundhouse, and we were curious to see the building up close.

We walked slowly through the center of town until we came to the roundhouse. It was almost as big as the Ogden train station, and its immense doors stood thirty feet tall. There was a locomotive inside on the turntable, and because the building was so immense, it made the huge train engine look miniscule.

There were dozens of workers dressed in striped coveralls throughout the building. We entered, but before we had gone more than a couple of feet, a large Negro man in blue coveralls raced over to intercept us. He was obviously angry and wanted to know what we were doing inside the building. I was caught off guard, so I just extended my hand and introduced myself as a new permanent employee of UP. I mentioned that Mr. Brown had suggested that we familiarize ourselves with the town.

The big man softened his frown, removed his large oil-stained glove, and shook my hand. He welcomed me but avoided looking at Gretchen.

"Occasionally, pilgrims get off a train and aimlessly wander into the building. We workers have all been instructed to run 'em off. The bad publicity to the railroad is too great if a person gets hurt here," the man said.

He told me that I was welcome anytime, but women and children weren't allowed inside the roundhouse. The man nervously but politely tipped his cap to Gretchen and asked her to please leave. "It is bad luck for a woman to be inside this building!"

Gretchen could see fine from the open doorway, and although it surprised her, she understood and didn't want to make any trouble for me. She was gracious and gently pushed me forward so I could accompany the huge man on the tour. I felt foolish, but Gretchen just smiled and reassured me that she wasn't unhappy.

As I walked with the man around the building, I could see her waiting patiently outside the open doorway. I knew that she could see everything from the doorway, but it concerned me that she couldn't come inside—but it didn't bother me enough to get myself fired before I even started work. When I returned, I tried to offer excuses for the engineer's behavior, but Gretchen just shook it off.

She told me, "Samuel, it's a man's world, and I am more than used to it by now. You just love me, and I can live with any of their restrictions and superstitions."

We continued our familiarization tour through Logo, but since we didn't know what we were looking at, we made the decision to return to our house. We would explore them at another time after I learned all of the rules of protocol.

As we passed the store, Gretchen noticed another building near the apartment complex. Neither of us had noticed it previously. The building was long and narrow with numbered doors. We didn't have to wait to find the answer because just then, Seth was leaving the store and saw us looking at the building.

Without asking, he volunteered an answer. "That is a flophouse of sorts. Workers who are delayed here for a while are billeted into those quarters. Each room has one canvas bed, a pillow, sheet, blanket, some towels, a small table, and one chair. The toilets and showers are on the end of the row. If someone has to be here for a few hours, UP doesn't want these men malingering in the store or wandering around the town. They are assigned a numbered room and told to stay in their rooms until notified by an engineer to board the train. They nap, catch a bite to eat, occasionally sip some wine, but that's about it. Anyone who overdoes the alcohol need not go back to the train—they are unemployed. The people who stay there don't have much of a social life while in Logo."

As it happened, we were in front of the store when a train arrived. Seth asked us to wait while he checked to see if more of our caboose community families were aboard. While we were waiting, I raced into the store, and using $2.25 of the allowance money Gretchen had given me, I purchased some milk, a box of oatmeal, and some crackers. That would tide us over until we could make up a grocery list. I was thankful that I hadn't listened to Gretchen's advice and tied my change in a handkerchief.

Seconds later, Seth appeared from around the building leading several couples and a gaggle of children. Seth led them to where Gretchen and I were standing. He introduced the people to us and told them that we were the people who were going to help them get settled. Gretchen and I shook their hands, and now being the "old-timers," we assumed responsibility for welcoming the new arrivals. We helped them carry their infant children and their belongings to their new homes.

We assembled the group in the street and told them everything we could remember about their new quarters. We tried to convey our excitement to help them with the adjustment. We invited everyone to come to our unit the next morning and help us eat a meager breakfast. We all agreed to meet at eight. No one refused.

The twelve cabooses stretched in a line from west to east. I assigned couples with children to the western units. Grouping families together would help with group child care. We were happy to be here, but Gretchen was looking pooped.

Gretchen was very tired and has now retired for the night. I am using this quiet time to record the events of the day while the details are still fresh in my mind. Tomorrow is Saturday, and we will use much of the day to rest and recuperate. The rest of our caboose community is scheduled to arrive sometime tomorrow.

May 14, 1921 (Saturday)
Gretchen got up early and used most of our pots and pans to heat up a huge batch of oatmeal and milk. By the time we were ready to eat, nineteen of us had crowded into our unit—twelve adults, five children, and two infants. Surprisingly, there was actually room for all of us. When we were assembled, our Norwegian neighbor, Mrs. Larsen, offered to say a blessing on the food.

The Larsen family was originally from Norway but had lived in Minnesota with relatives for the past two years and had applied for US citizenship. Lars speaks very little English, but his wife Bertha is fluent. Between the two they are going to be okay. Lars will learn from his wife and from his coworkers what he needs to know. He made an attempt to speak to Gretchen and me.

"Hi, I yam Lars Larssen, I yam from Meee-nah-sow-tah. I no spik Engleesh soo goot. 'appy to met ya."

Lars and Bertha were both large people. Lars was wide, tall, bearded, and strong. Bertha was almost as wide as she was tall. A happier couple I had never seen. The Larsen luggage consisted of one large steamer trunk and a banjo.

"I need to mention that over the next five years, Dad and Lars became the best of friends," Bill added.

The small children were mostly infants in arms, so they didn't create a mess or make much noise. We all sat around our caboose wherever we could find a spot. No one seemed to want to eat outside. Once during breakfast, Mrs. Larsen spoke to Gretchen in her right ear. It became immediately obvious to her that Gretchen was partially deaf. She and the other adults adjusted their speech volume and direction. Gretchen never even noticed the discreet change in the conversation.

After breakfast, Gretchen visited with the women while the men accompanied me on a trip around town. I explained the restrictions in the roundhouse. Lars couldn't understand much of the conversation, so I stayed close by him and did a lot of pointing and smiling. He caught just enough to get an idea of what I was talking about.

We were able to go inside one of the helper buildings, and one of the engineers was polite and helpful. He even let each of us climb into the vehicle and sit in the engineer's chair. One man asked if he could blow the whistle, but the engineer explained it only worked when the boiler was fired up. Even then it was discouraged because it made so much noise in the confined space of the building.

We went through the roundhouse, looked at the engineer's quarters and the flophouses, and pointed out the transient quarters. I relayed what Mr. Brown had said and advised them to leave those men alone. We then returned to our units.

At noon, the last six couples arrived, but by this time, the welcoming committee was comprised of every member of our caboose community, plus the Browns.

Mr. Brown introduced himself to the new arrivals and then introduced Gretchen and me. I surprised myself when I was able to put the correct names of the community members with the applicable faces. Mr. Brown turned the group over to Gretchen and me. Mr. Brown wasn't shirking his duty; it was just his way of letting all of us get acquainted. In this new group, we had three veterans who had just returned from fighting the Germans in France.

Four of the couples had children, so I assigned them units that were near the other couples with children. No one questioned me or seemed disappointed in where they were assigned. It was settled, and the workers and their families knew where they would be living for the next five years. By late afternoon, all twelve cabooses were occupied.

The oldest resident of this new community was twenty-eight and had three children. The youngest adult residents were Jake and Tina Bedford. She was a tiny, frail sixteen-year-old girl with a newborn baby. Jake hadn't yet turned eighteen, but he had already assumed the responsibility of being a husband and father.

It took a few minutes for the families to get moved in, and then I asked the entire group to assemble outside.

The oldest youngster in the community was seven years old. That kid was going to be the self-appointed leader and official authority on everything.

Because I had been the person who seemed to know what was going on, I became the nonelected mayor of the community. I led them into the backyard that had been staked out by UP for gardens. I pointed to the four strategically placed water pumps. At that point, I was unquestionably the lead authority. I explained to the group that we were going to be together for a long time, and I thought it might be well for us to pool our seed and sweat and plant a garden. We could then share in the harvest. I explained that if we worked together, we could save more money to help us start our own farms. No one objected to the plan.

After riding buggies and trains most of the day, people wanted to take a bath. The women needed to care for their children. The young ones needed feeding, especially the newborns. The units were clean, but not to the satisfaction of these women. These good ladies would take soap and water and start over.

All of the families had a couple of things in common. First, we were all on the low end of the working class, but now could see a way to improve our lives. The second thing was that we all wanted homes and this job would provide us with the cash and the land. It was the future for us!

Mr. Brown had told me that we all needed to be at the store by seven o'clock on Monday morning. I let the workers know that they didn't need to bring a lunch, but they should be dressed for work and bring along a good pair of work gloves.

I went with the new men and explained what I knew of the roundhouse and the special rules and regulations.

We returned an hour later just in time to dig into a potluck lunch. The women had hauled chairs and benches out of the units and positioned them in a circle outside. The meal consisted of what food was left over in the various picnic baskets or pantries.

We had no meat but plenty of fruits and vegetables. After everyone had eaten, I again addressed the group and suggested that we might pool our resources and buy enough food to feed us until we got our first paycheck. I suggested that we put in one dollar per person. People came forward and put currency and coin into my hat. Two of the families were deeply embarrassed—they simply didn't have any money. Tina Bedford, the young mother with the newborn, suddenly stepped forward and put a ten dollar bill into the hat. Smiling, she looked at the two financially strapped families. "You can pay me back when you get your paycheck," she said. Nothing more was said, but this young lady earned a new respect from the entire group.

I didn't count the cash. I just handed it to Jake and asked him to purchase as much food as the money would buy. Two men went with him to help carry the grocery items.

An hour later, the men returned pulling a large baggage wagon filled with groceries. The wagon was packed to overflowing with flour, salt, sugar, and other dry goods. I couldn't imagine how Jake was able to get that much food for such a small amount of money. The three men were smiling, but it was evident they were fighting back tears.

Jake was the first to speak. "Mr. Brown wouldn't take our money. He told us that our first two weeks food was on him. We tried to get him to take what we had, but he refused. He explained that UP employees were afforded a store discount, but in the future, we shouldn't expect our discount to be quite as large as this one."

When the food was spread out, the contents included beef, pork, milk, eggs, flour, salt, coffee, fresh fruits, yeast, and fresh vegetables. There was even condensed milk for the babies.

Gretchen clasped her hands together and loudly exclaimed, "Homemade bread! We are going to have homemade bread! Now someone here has to teach me how to make it." The adults all laughed.

The money was returned to each of the donors, and a lot of tears of gratitude were shed.

Later in the day, Gretchen and I took a stroll and ended up at the store—we also wanted to thank Mr. Brown on behalf of the group for his generosity.

As I was standing near the diner talking to Seth, I read the menu aloud. Putting my arm around Gretchen, I announced to Seth that someday I was going to bring my sweet wife into his eatery and buy her the biggest steak in the place.

Seth had no way of knowing, but neither of us had ever eaten a meal in a restaurant, let alone a steak. And with the exception of an occasional church get-together, neither of us had ever eaten a meal cooked by anyone other than us or our parents. We had never been invited to a neighbor's home for a Sunday dinner. This was going to be a real treat, and Gretchen was visibly overjoyed at the thought.

Mr. Brown slapped my shoulder and told me that he would make sure it was the biggest, most tender, delicious steak he had ever prepared.

Before the group retired for the evening, I let everyone know about church services that would be held the next morning. I assured them that attendance was optional.

Bill added more to the story. "Dad explained to me that passenger and freight trains made short stops in Logo, primarily to get water and fuel. The stops allowed passengers, workers, and the engineers to get off the train long enough to stretch their legs and to purchase a meal. When the train was ready to leave, it would blow its whistle twice, and workers and passengers would know that the train would leave in five minutes.

"Every building in Logo had been constructed by UP. The Browns had been hired to manage the store and diner, serve as paymasters, greeters, postmasters, ticket agents, and resident medical staff. They loved the work, and the people who lived there loved and respected them. The passengers and crew knew that they could get a quality meal at a fair price. Both of the Browns were exceptionally good cooks; their boys, ages sixteen and seventeen, were learning but hadn't mastered the finites. They could cook a good hamburger, but the great meals came from the hands and minds of the senior Browns."

May 15, 1921 (Sunday)
We got up this morning, finished off the sack of oatmeal, and headed for church. Somewhat to my surprise, everyone who lived in our community came to church. They must have all felt especially grateful this particular Sunday. There were about seventy people in attendance, and the room was barely large enough to accommodate us. Several men stood in the back because there were not enough chairs.

Mr. Brown welcomed us to church and told us that the seating shortage problem would be corrected before next Sunday.

"Since we don't have a minister, it will be up to us to decide if we want to share some inspirational thoughts with the congregation," Mr. Brown said.

"I have asked Mrs. Burns to give us an opening prayer, and she will also lead us in singing 'Rock of Ages.' If you don't know the words, just hum along," Mr. Brown added.

It was indeed a multidenominational service. There was no minister, hymnals, or musical instruments. Some attendees said silent prayers, others fingered beads, but each person worshiped in their own way.

After the prayer and song, most of the men standing in the back left the meeting. They didn't want to stand while being reminded of their sins. It would be bad enough to be chastised by their wives after they got home.

Mrs. Brown was the first to stand. She walked to the front of the room near the blackboard and stood behind Mrs. Harwood's desk.

"I am grateful for the opportunity to live in this blessed land. I am grateful to be able to worship God in my own way and to be provided with food, clothing, shelter, and divine protection. I am thankful to associate with you fine folks, and I want to welcome all of the new UP employees to these Sabbath services."

I didn't know any better, so I applauded. Most of the people in the room wrinkled their foreheads and looked at me like I was a dunce. Gretchen stroked the hair on the back of my head and smiled at me.

Mr. Brown stood and read several verses of scripture from the Bible and then sat down. No one else stood up, and the silence was deafening. For some unknown reason, I got to my feet and walked up behind the desk and shared a few of my feelings with the group.

Bill again interjected. "In the packet in the back of Dad's journal, there was a handwritten sheet written by Mrs. Brown. She was touched and wrote down the text of Dad's testimony of gratitude. This is what she wrote."

> This is my first church meeting with you good neighbors and one of the few times I have ever stood up to speak before a congregation, but I feel I need to share something with you. I want to talk about gratitude. I have had little in this life by way of material things. I have always been poor, and it is a way of life for me. The best thing that ever happened to me was when Gretchen agreed to be my wife. Now, suddenly, my wife and I have been given a wonderful opportunity to better ourselves. I publicly want to thank God for seeing our needs and to UP for their trust and for giving us the means to get out of the trench that I have been in my entire life. Also, I promise not to applaud if anyone else has something to say. I have learned my lesson.

Bill then mentioned, "Dad also said, 'I knew that most of the people who lived in the caboose community were in about the same financial shape as Gretchen and me, but I wanted them to know that there was hope.'"

> A few of the engineers' wives stood, but most of the caboose tenants were so choked up with emotion, they could barely utter a word.
>
> Two of the wives of the engineers stood and quoted a few lines of scriptures primarily relating to brotherly love. Their hollow words came from their mouths, not from their hearts. Their husbands had good jobs. These women probably never had to forego the pleasures of life. They wore beautiful clothing, rings, jewelry, and elegant hats. I was trying not to judge them, but I understood humility, and these women didn't have any. It came time for the hymn and a closing prayer.

To my surprise and horror, Mr. Brown then asked me to offer the closing prayer. I had never said a public prayer in my life. I tried frantically to recall the words of the opening prayer, but my mind went blank. I said a prayer, and when I was finished, I waved thanks to my neighbors, walked back to my seat, and sat down. Gretchen smiled and patted me on my knee. Services closed, and we walked back to our units.

"Dad later told me that he couldn't refuse, so he stood and did the best he could. After a little prodding, he finally repeated to me what he said in his prayer. It might be a little off, but it is basically correct. As you noticed, he didn't record it in his journal other than to say he prayed."

Heavenly Father, thank You for helping all of us in our time of need. We are all down, and we need someone to lean on, so I guess that has to be You. Help us to be honorable people and do a good job for UP. That's about it, Lord. Amen."

Bill again interjected, "It was a simple prayer, but it must have touched people because of its sincerity. I am confident that it gave people cause to reflect and be thankful for the opportunities that had been given them.

"My father found it interesting that for the entire five years, few discussions were ever made by the other Caboosers without first asking him for advice. He hadn't campaigned for anything like that. It just happened because they respected him. He had somehow become the father figure, and it was a foregone conclusion that his word was law. He told me that he has never had that kind of authority or trust before or since."

Working on the Railroad

On Monday, the workers met and received their week's work schedule and were assigned pigeonhole mailboxes. The schedule simply said that they were to be on the dock, ready to go to work at 7:00 a.m., Monday through Saturday. This particular Monday was an exception.

I stood facing the loading platform with my coworkers. Our wives and other family members huddled together in the shade of the nearby railway station. Bertha Larsen came with Lars so that she could interpret and relay important information. None of us knew what to expect. The only thing we knew was that we were supposed to be there by eight. At the exact time when the railroad clock chimed, a distinguished-looking man walked to the edge of the platform.

"My name is Melvin Stanford, and I will be your general supervisor for the next five years, unless, of course, the good Lord decides to take me or one of you before then. You all should know that my mother, my wife, and the president of UP call me Melvin, but no one else. To you, I am Mr. Stanford, and whether I am within earshot or a hundred miles away, that is what I will be called.

"I want your work to be enjoyable, but you must know from the onset that it will be hard, and you will know that you have earned your pay. You will spend this first month working on the rails with pick and shovel. I want you to know what it takes to build a railway. Since most of you will be with us for five years, I would expect you to move ahead and assume greater responsibilities. Consider this on-the-job training. You can't supervise others if you don't know how to do the work or be able to recognize a worker's physical or mental limitations.

"The work is hard, so you will need to know how much you can take and what you can expect of others. Don't kill yourselves trying to impress me—it won't work. I've been doing this type of work since before most of you were born. I know how far to push you before you lose your effectiveness and initiative. You need to know how far to push others. We need to put down track over a two-hundred-mile stretch, and that isn't an easy task, especially in the mountains.

"This company is fair, and all we expect is a day's work for a day's pay. You will need breaks, and they will be provided. We want you to have some energy left when you come home to your family. They deserve your love and attention. We won't take that from you. The last half hour will be used to perform easier tasks. When you hop off the train in the evening, you rush home. Don't linger and figure you'll play a few games of cards or have a drink. Your wives deserve better. If you can't get along with your wives, then you won't be able to get along with UP or me!

Mr. Stanford paused long enough for his words to sink in. He then began to pace the full length of the dock making eye contact with all of the workers.

"Another thing—I hate profanity almost as much as I hate drunkenness. You might get away with a cuss word in front of me once, but don't expect it to be ignored a second time. I will embarrass you in front of your friends and coworkers, and trust me when I tell you, that I can be ruthless when I get riled. Don't swear at each other, the weather, spikes, rails, shovels, blisters, bugs, or your employer. Follow this counsel, and you will be better men because of it.

"You will be working six ten-hour days, but you will receive overtime pay for Saturday work. It doesn't impact the length of your contract, but it will give you more money than you had expected. You will receive your pay in cash on the first workday of the month. You are not going to be paid in advance, so don't ask me about it.

"Every other month, you will be given one Saturday off with pay. No more than six workers will be gone at the same time, so don't plan group vacations. On that day off, you will be given regular pay, not overtime.

He stopped pacing and stood directly in front of the wives and children. He locked his hands behind his back, smiled, and looked directly at them before he spoke.

"Workers and their families can ride the train at no cost. Once you get to Ogden, the lines connect several other cities. But regardless of where you go, you make sure that you get your husbands back here in time for work on Monday. It is essential that they do not return late or miss work.

He then paced back to the center of the platform making eye contact with both the workers and the family members.

"At some future time, you will be given exact work schedules, but for the present you will report here at seven o'clock in the morning, ready for work. Currently, we will be setting track southward toward Salt Lake City. The mountains will make it difficult to progress more than a few miles a week. Spurs need to be built to connect towns and for temporary bypasses. Summers will present problems with heat, bugs, and snakes. Winters will be windy and cold.

"If for any reason you become ill or have some other serious problem, then you or your missus must notify Mr. Brown. He is your contact point. If you oversleep and miss your work train, you will have a strike against you. Think twice about missing the train again because your third miss will result in your contract being terminated. If you plan on missing the train three times, it had better happen two days before your contract is up.

"I thank you for your attention. Do any of you have any relative questions?"

A hand shot into the air. "Mr. Stanford, do we bring our lunch, or is food provided?"

"You will be provided with coffee, water, and juice during the day. One half hour is scheduled each day for you to eat. Your luncheon meal will be provided, and it will be quality food. It is prepared at the Brown diner, and they are very good cooks. This meal is at no cost to you, but you are not to bring food home to your families. What chow isn't eaten at the work site will be given to homeless people along the railway route. It builds good community relations. You each have been given a family grocery allowance, and we expect you to use that money to cover your food needs. Let me again emphasize, don't even bring an apple home. It will be treated as theft and would be a violation of your contract, and you will probably be terminated. Betting one stale leftover apple against your parcel of land is a bad gamble. I hope you understand what I am saying because it is important!

"You will all have enough time to eat your food, but do not go to sleep. You may relax and rest in the shade of a tree or a boxcar, but sleeping on the job is prohibited. You are paid for ten hours of work, and your noon break is figured into those ten hours. You are transported to and from the job, and that transportation time is also counted toward your ten-hour day. We are fair with you and expect you to be fair with UP."

Another hand was raised. "Mr. Stanford, do we need to furnish any of our own tools?"

"No," Mr. Stanford responded. "We provide everything you need except clothing and gloves. If you think you are going to get cold, then bring a coat. If blisters and sunburns don't bother you, then you can work partially naked for all I care, but I recommend against it. If any of you get a hangover or sunburn that prevents you from performing your work, it will be considered destruction of UP property, and for the next five years, you are UP property." He said this without even cracking a smile.

Everyone quietly snickered.
"Some people can work on a pick and shovel and never get a blister. I am not one of those fortunate souls. I wear the best gloves I can buy. Mr. Brown has an excellent selection of quality gloves in his store. Personally, I would recommend that you buy the best grade leather gloves he has. Are there any more questions, pertinent questions?"

From the back of the group, a hand was raised and Mr. Sanford acknowledged him. "There are a lot of deer and fowl around here. On our day off, can we go hunting?"

Without even looking directly at the man, he responded, "No." He paused, and when no more hands were raised, he continued. "Then I bid you a good day. Hop on the flatbed and find a place to sit. We will be traveling about ten miles this morning at roughly thirty miles per hour. The trip will take about twenty minutes, so I would suggest that you hang on to the ropes and the rings located in the center of the flatbed. Your widow receives nothing if you fall off the train, and it is difficult and time-consuming to clean excess skin, crushed bones, and blood off the tracks and grade.

"I will be up front with the engineer sitting in a comfortably padded chair protected from wind and dust. I will probably have a cold glass of lemonade in my hand. I have been with the railroad for thirty-eight years, and one of the things I have earned with my seniority is that I no longer have to ride on the flatbed!"

He laughed and waved, and we laughed with him.

This man seemed to have a sense of humor, and we now knew what he expected of us. We would work hard for him.

Bertha Larsen was almost out of breath when Mr. Stanford finished speaking. She had stood far enough away from the rest of us so that her interpretation efforts for Lars wouldn't distract anyone.

While the men were climbing aboard the flatbed, Mr. Stanford walked over to Bertha, smiled, and gently shook her hand. "You needn't worry about your husband because the railhead foreman is from Oslo."

Bertha gave a sigh of relief and gratefully clasped Mr. Stanford's hands in both of hers.

The ride was rough but not unbearable. Flatbed cars are made with hardwood decks and heavy-duty springs intended for supporting very heavy loads, so even the short ten-mile ride was tough on the bottom. Being mid-May, the air and breeze were chilly, so we clustered together for warmth but all the while keeping a firm hold on the safety ropes.

As Mr. Stanford had predicted, the trip took exactly twenty minutes. We were met by a tall, balding, bulky man with a handlebar mustache. Patches of dark-black body hair protruded through holes in his sleeveless tobacco-stained shirt.

He pointed to an area where we were to assemble. To the side we could see about forty other workers already huddled together armed with picks, shovels, and rakes.

"My name is Sherwood Pyle, and I am the loading and rail-grade preparation foreman. For the next two weeks, you twelve men will be working as a team and are mine, body and soul."

We were delighted to learn that we would be working together but weren't so sure about the rest of the arrangements.

Mr. Pyle again spoke. "Heavy equipment has already done the hard part of carving out the route. All you men will do is follow the excavation and do the easy part of removing rock, brush, tree roots, and other objects that the graders may have missed. Where you find low spots, you will use your shovels and fill those spots with rocks and soil. High spots will be cut down to size with picks, shovels, and crowbars. When the superintendent is satisfied that the grade is firm and level, he will give the go-ahead to apply bed gravel. For the next two weeks, along with your other duties, you will be raking, shoveling, and smoothing gravel. Two weeks after that you will be laying track.

"I will be supervising your work and will be close by to answer questions and direct your activity. You gentlemen are soon going to develop muscles you never knew you had and will also acquire some on-the-job training in the use of some of the oldest instruments known to man, the pick and shovel."

The foreman motioned for us to follow him.
"Grab a pick, shovel, rake, or crowbar. It won't matter what you select because you will all be switching tools back and forth during the day. I trust that you have good gloves, but if you don't, I will loan you a pair for today only.
"Because we are working in mountains, we can't use the same grading equipment we used to clear a rail route through the flatlands. You men are the replacements for that grading and leveling equipment. Mr. Stanford has already told you what to expect, so let's not disappoint him."

The twelve of us picked up our tools and followed the foreman about six hundred feet to the end of the finished track. Mr. Pyle stopped abruptly and pointed to a pile of rock.
"This is where the track crew will start their work. To be out of their way, we will begin our work about a thousand feet farther down the line. The work will be difficult, and we don't want any of you getting sunstroke.

Work at a steady pace. When I blow my whistle, you stop and take a ten-minute break.

"You will learn how to prepare a grade, but you will also learn to recognize how much strenuous work you can do before you become ineffective. That knowledge will help you when you have work crews working under you. You need to recognize physical limitations of yourselves and your people before you can be a good supervisor. Exhausted workers become ineffective and make errors.

"There aren't toilets, so it is up to you to find a place to relieve yourselves. When you leave the group, let a member of your team know you are going and take a shovel with you and bury the evidence. Also, a shovel is a good protection against rattlers, and there are a lot of them around."

At noontime, one of Mr. Brown's sons appeared in the distance driving a one-horse milk wagon. Mr. Pyle's whistle sounded, and he shouted for us to come to the wagon and get our lunch.

None of us knew what we would be eating, but we had assumed it would be the same food that had sustained the earlier railroad workers—beans, bacon, hardtack, and buffalo jerky. Instead, we were pleasantly surprised to be served homemade bread and delicious lunch, and then we topped it off with crisp apples and pears. I found some shade under a mahogany tree, and after checking for snakes, I sat down with my back against the tree and relaxed, grateful for the brief work respite.

The work after lunch was harder than I would have imagined. The sun beat down, and I was sweating and feeling lightheaded. The foreman had apparently noticed my condition because he again blew his whistle and told all of us to get a drink and rest for ten minutes.

Mules laden with water bags were always nearby, so we never lacked for water. We were advised to drink often but sparingly to avoid getting stomach cramps.

Three hours later, the blessed whistle sounded, and Mr. Pyle instructed us to put our tools in the overnight storage shed. I slowly stood erect and flexed my aching neck and shoulder muscles while at the same time rubbing my lower back. None of us had to be coaxed to follow the foreman away from the grading site.

As Mr. Stanford had promised, the last half hour of work was much easier. Some of the men painted wooden ties with oil and creosote while others scraped rust and hardened mud from the rails while others took inventory. It was all work that had to be done, but it didn't take a strong back or mind to do it.

The ride home was a welcome end to a long workday. We were all tired, but the wind in our faces was refreshing. When we got to Logo, I was surprised and delighted to see Gretchen standing on the dock along with all of the other wives and children. I felt like a veteran returning from serving in a foreign war, and I figured the rest of us shared the same feeling.

My aches, pains, and fatigue seemed to magically disappear, and I was refreshed and energized beyond belief.

Gretchen and I walked hand in hand along with the others to our boxcar havens. We said good-bye to the others and went inside.

When Gretchen held me in her arms and kissed me, it was at that moment that I was sure that I would be able to make it for the full five years.

May 30, 1921 (Monday)

After two weeks of repetitive line work, we were turned over to Mr. Ernstrom. He met us first thing this morning and asked us to all gather around him.

"My name is Jon Kristen Ernstrom, and most of us have informally met. I am the track boss and will be directing your work for the next two weeks."

Next to me, Lars was smiling. Mr. Ernstrom had spoken to him before in his native Norwegian. Lars finally had someone who could give him instructions he could understand.

The foreman continued. "Each morning, you men have passed by the track crew on your way to your somewhat-relaxing job."

Everyone laughed.

"Today, you will find out what real work is. I could talk to you for days about what we are going to do, but I feel that ten minutes of work will show you. All the tools you will need are stored at the site, so follow me, and we can go have some physical fun."

Stopping near the end of the completed track, he motioned for us to watch him as he placed his foot between ties.

"My foot is eleven inches long. The distance between ties is ten inches. By butting the heel of my shoe up against a tie, I can judge the approximate position where the next tie will be placed. If your foot is exactly ten inches long, then you have an advantage over the rest of us. If you have extraordinarily big feet, like Lars Larsen, then you can measure by using the width of the shoe rather than the length," the foreman joked.

Everyone laughed and looked at Lars. Directing his attention to Lars, he repeated in Norwegian what he had just said. Lars got a grin on his face and blushed.

The foreman spoke again. "The measurement doesn't have to be precise, but it should be a close approximation. Ties placed too close together represent an added expense. Ties placed a greater distance than ten inches could present a future hazard. Anyway, about every thirty feet, I will make sure we don't compound a tie-positioning error."

Certain that we understood, with a forward sweep of his arm, he motioned for us to get to work.

"Okay, you all have had enough down time. Now it is time to lay some track."

We immediately began to move the heavy ties from the stack to the grade. My muscles ached, but as a group, I thought we were working well together.

When one hundred ties had been positioned, the foreman had us stop work while he and a surveyor worked together to align the placed ties. Two men were selected to either raise or lower those ties that were out of position. I was not one of the men selected, so the brief rest was appreciated.

The surveyor nodded, and the foreman motioned with his fingers for us to bring up six rails and place them on the chalk marks he had made on the ties. He divided us into eight-man teams, and under his direction, we worked together to manually position one of the heavy rails into place. When the six rails had been seated, the surveyor, satisfied with the alignment, nodded to our foreman to proceed, and we repeated the process.

Our next job was to drive the spikes into place. I soon found that driving a spike with a small-headed spike mallet is quite an adventure in timing and skill. My first swing was a complete miss, but after a dozen or so more attempts, I mastered the timing. Soon I was swinging as well as most of the other workers, except for Lars. Lars must have been born with a mallet in his hand because he worked circles around the rest of us. Ten minutes after he took his first swing, he was driving three spikes to my one.

Over the next six hours, we put down three hundred feet of track and were pretty pleased with our accomplishment. The track superintendent inspected our work and gave us authority to continue. We were rather happy, but our joy was short-lived when the foreman told us that we were behind schedule and needed to put in one hundred feet in the next two hours to get back on schedule.

The foreman explained that he had been charged with the responsibility of laying no less than four hundred feet of track per day, and he was determined that he would make or beat the goal.

June 20, 1921 (Monday)
Today we started our fifth week, and it was an exciting day.

Upon arriving at the railhead, we were met again by Sherwood Pyle, our beloved rotund tobacco-chewing line boss. I would swear that he was still wearing the same stained shirt he had on two weeks ago. We knew what he expected of us, so there would be no surprises. He had us form in a line, and then he filled us in on our new duty assignments.

"You gentlemen are going to learn some new skills. Most likely, the job you are assigned today, you will be doing for the rest of your contract. It will be less strenuous than the work you have been doing these past four weeks, but there will still be physical labor involved. Some of you will be wagon drivers, and the rest will be loaders."

He walked down the line and made work assignments. When he came to me, he told me that I would be a driver and the straw boss for the group. Lars was selected to be a loader.

"Now that you know your function, I want to take a few minutes to tell you how this operation works. Pay attention because I don't have time to repeat myself," the foreman said.

"Yonder you can see seven flatbed railcars loaded with ties, rails, spikes, and other machinery. Farther down adjacent to the tracks are the horse stables. On a normal day, the stables will house at least twenty animals, and there will be a dozen or so empty wagons of various sizes, greased and ready to go. The wagons used to transport ties are pulled by two horses. The load weight is the maximum the animals can pull, so we never overload them. The longer wagons with the extended beds are used to transport rails.

"The rails are thirty-three feet long, and it takes eight strong men to move one heavy steel rail. It takes one of the long-bed wagons to take a load of rails, and the number of rails on any one wagon will be determined by the loading boss, not by you workers. The ties are also heavy. They are eight feet long and weigh about 120 pounds each. Understand that it will take two strong men to lift one.

"A team will never be hitched to a wagon until it is fully loaded. We can't take the chance of spooking and injuring one of the animals. The hitching process will be performed by mule skinners. You may be tempted to offer advice and assistance, but don't do it. The skinners are a surly bunch who knows what they are doing. You keep out of their way and leave them alone.

"It takes approximately five hundred ties and thirty rails to complete a four-hundred-foot section of track. Your responsibility is to keep ahead of the track crew. You can usually do it by making four hauls a day."

Lars stood next to me and smiled when I smiled and nodded when I nodded. He had absolutely no idea what was being said. Over the last four weeks, he had learned enough English to comprehend a word or two, but a full sentence was far beyond him. He could create a rough sentence much better than he could understand one.

"After you load your wagons, the skinners will take over and hitch up the team. They will form the six wagons into a line, and you won't take over until the mule skinner gives the reins to you.

"Nobody is to move a wagon until I give the go-ahead. When you return, the skinners will have already put empty wagons next to the flatbeds. All you have to do is set your wagon brake and wait for a skinner to come to you. When he tells you, give him the reins and go start loading your new wagon. Help each other. Remember, those ties and rails are heavy, and the loading will be easier and will go faster if you all work together," the foreman said.

The line boss put his hand on my shoulder and spoke loudly enough for everyone to hear. "Samuel Spader will be your straw boss. Where he goes, you follow. After the wagons are unloaded, he will lead you back here. Don't head off on your own. Always coordinate all your travel with Samuel.

"Each driver will have one loader assigned to him. The driver may choose his loader if he has a preference. Personally, I would pick the strongest man," he joked.

I gave a head jerk motion to Lars, and he raced to my side. He also happened to be the strongest person in the work crew.

"We expect you to make a minimum of two trips before noon and another two trips after you chow down. In the past, you have eaten at your workstation, but from now on, you will eat your meals here. Besides, the food here is better," he observed.

"Regardless of when you complete your second trip, you are to go directly to the flatbed and get something to eat. You will have thirty minutes, but go easy on the liquids. You can drink small amounts often, but drinking too much too fast can sap your energy and make you ill. Also, taking a couple of pinches of salt with your meal will help you retain moisture in your body.

"Another thing—never under any circumstance are you to overload the wagons. Limit loads to one hundred ties on the smaller wagons and thirty rails on the extended bed wagons," he firmly admonished. "More weight can ruin the wagon or, more importantly, can injure an animal."

When the foreman was through giving instructions, he hopped onto one of the flatbeds and demonstrated the loading process. We all climbed aboard the flatbeds and started loading while the foreman went from flatbed to flatbed to make sure we were loading exactly the right number of ties or rails onto the wagons.

As soon as the wagons were loaded to the satisfaction of our foreman, he gave a hand signal, and the mule skinners backed their horses next to the wagon tongues. The skinners worked quickly and efficiently. Once the teams were hitched, the skinners hopped up on the bench seat and formed the six wagons into a line. When the wagons were in position, the foreman spoke directly to me but bellowed his instructions so that everyone could hear.

"Make sure you and the other drivers check in with the track foreman before you unload. When you are finished, you all come back here together. I will expect to see you here in less than two hours!"

Not one of us owned a wrist or pocket watch, so we would have to work quickly and hope for the best.

The foreman gave me the go-ahead to move out. I waved my arm forward, and the rest of the wagon train followed.

It took about twenty minutes to get to the end of track. I didn't have to locate him because he saw us coming and was waiting at the side of the trail.

"Well, I see you two finally got a cushy job," he said.

Mr. Ernstrom again gave Lars a friendly Norwegian greeting, and Lars responded back. They both smiled. The foreman waited until all of his crew had assembled around him.

"I want the ties stacked every hundred feet. Find a flat place to unload and stack them. If you can't find a flat place, then use your picks and shovels and make one. The tools are attached to the sides of the wagons. Place the rails parallel to the grade but not on it. Six rails are needed for every one hundred feet of ties.

"You have taken down my tie stacks before, so now you can learn how to build them. I want them placed in groups of ten. Put ten on the bottom with a space of four inches between ties. Crisscross the next level with the same spacing until the stack is about eight feet tall. One stack contains one hundred ties, so your wagon should be empty when you are finished."

Speaking to me but again so that the others could hear, he said, "You have obviously noticed the noise in the left front wheel. There is nothing wrong with the wheel. A clapper has been installed that will make a noise with each completed revolution. One click represents about fifteen feet. Keep driving, and after the seventh click, Spader here will raise his hand and let the last wagon driver know that he should stop. The rail wagon should also stop, and you men can unload six rails. Each time a tie wagon stops, the rail wagon should also stop. Make sure that before the driver ever gets off the wagon that his horse or horses are hobbled. When a wagon is empty, it should be parked with the brakes set. You men then help the others unload and stack. When the ties are all stacked, you can hitch a ride back to your own wagon before heading back here.

"Mr. Spader will always be in the lead, so follow him. Check with me before you leave in case I have people or equipment I want you to haul back."

The foreman then gently slapped the rump of our horse, and it moved forward.

We clicked along, Lars counting aloud in Norwegian. I was grateful that we weren't going far. On the next trip I will make sure he counts silently.

I pointed to a relatively flat place and gestured with my hands that the spot needed to be more level. Lars jumped from the wagon and grabbed a shovel and rake. It only took a few minutes for him to prepare a spot for the ties. I set the brake on the wagon and held the reins firmly while Lars worked.

When he was satisfied, he motioned, and I backed up the wagon and set the brakes while Lars hobbled the horses. We were about half through unloading and stacking when the rail wagon and the rest of our group arrived. The work went quickly, and about ten minutes later, the crew hopped into the empty wagons, and we headed back. I didn't stop, and when a driver arrived in his empty wagon, he carefully pulled in behind our caravan.

In a loud voice that everyone could hear, he informed us that we were twenty minutes behind schedule.

When we got close to the train, I could see the empty wagons lined up next to the flatbed cars. I pulled into position, again set the wagon brake, and signaled to the skinners. When a skinner took the reins from me, I motion to Lars, and we headed for the flatbed. All twelve of us in our team worked together, and forty minutes later, we had all six wagons once again loaded and ready to go. The skinners hitched up the horses to the wagons, and we rested while they did their work. Within ten minutes, our caravan was ready to move out. Our second trip was organized, and we knew how to help one another. We had all wanted to make up the lost time and were pleased that we had picked up about fifteen minutes. Our empty bellies let us know that is was about time for lunch. The foreman must have been hungry also because he signaled for us to head back. Jon and two of his lead men ran alongside my wagon and hopped into the back.

"Let's go eat," Jon announced.

As we neared the loading area, we caught the smell of food.

The mule skinners were waiting, and they jumped onto our wagons before we even had time to come to a complete stop. Mr. Pyle greeted us and gave Jon a slap on his back and grinned.

The food was set out. We encircled Lars while he said a prayer. None of us knew what he said with the exception of Mr. Ernstrom, but at least we all knew we were eating blessed food.

We had expected to be eating sandwiches but were pleasantly surprised when we were served bowls of hot beef stew and fresh corn bread. There were fruits, fresh tomatoes, boiled eggs, cheeses, and for dessert, there was chocolate cake. This was far more than any of us had expected.

Jon glanced over at me and winked his eye. In his hands he cradled a steaming bowl of stew and a full plate of food. Now I knew why he never ate cold sandwiches in the field with the rest of our crew.

After we were through eating, we rested and visited for a while. When the line boss sounded his shrill whistle, we got up and went back to work.

The mule skinners had pushed the wagons into position, and we immediately started to load. Within forty minutes, we had all the wagons loaded with the correct number of ties or rails.

The skinners had again arranged the horses and wagons in a line, and we changed places with them on the padded driver's bench. Not one of those skinners said hello or even acknowledged us. These old skinners were a really independent and surly bunch.

Two minutes later, the foreman gave us the go-ahead, and we set out again, accompanied by Jon and his two lead men.

Sitting on a padded wagon sure beat swinging a pick!

The afternoon hauls were made much more quickly than they had been in the morning. We made up for lost time and ended the day ahead of schedule. Mr. Pyle appeared to be happy.

The ride home on the flatbed was actually refreshing. The wind on our faces felt cool and comforting. By the time I got to Logo, I was ready to have a nice evening with my wife.

Bonding

June 4, 1921 (Monday)

My sixth week of railroad work is now complete, and it has sure been a learning time for me. The work was difficult, but now I know what is expected, and those muscles of mine that used to constantly ache no longer hurt. I actually enjoy my newfound energy and strength.

Each day I become more familiar with Mr. Pyle and my work routine. We caboose workers all function as a team and actually compete with one another to see who can stack their ties in the best time. With experience comes efficiency.

One interesting thing happened yesterday that made the week more enjoyable. Lars Larsen brought his banjo with him. On the flatbed ride, Lars strummed away, and most of us sang or hummed along. He plays Norwegian folk songs, which none of us know, but he made an effort to play by ear a few of our country songs. He knows that we enjoy his music, so he will play while we finish our lunch. Mr. Pyle also seemed to enjoy the music because he let Lars go through the chow line first so that he can have more time to play. That gave us an opportunity to relax while we finished eating. The music settles us and keeps us awake. No one can sleep while listening to Lars rendition of "Camp Town Races."

At home, Gretchen spent the week cleaning the caboose and planting seeds in her precious garden.

Leave it to her to find out that the pay of all workers was the same, regardless of work assignment. We had all signed a contract and up front knew that we would be receiving one dollar per hour. It was a pleasant surprise to find out that on Saturday, we were to receive time and one-half pay.

"Dad recorded hundreds of things in his journal, but I will just touch on a few of them. There are several highlights, and I will either paraphrase or quote him, but what follows won't be in any specific date order, so I won't note the date when these events happened. One interesting item was how Mom used to siphon part of my father's paycheck without him knowing," Bill observed.

Per the terms of our contract, each worker was paid in cash on the first workday of the month. Since we are at work, we authorized our wives to pick up our pay. None of us knew exactly how much cash we had earned, but we were happy to have our wives pay the bills and do the bookkeeping.

It wasn't until my contract was over that I found out that Gretchen had been siphoning off forty dollars a month and stashing it away. She must have sewn it inside wearing apparel because I never discovered it. The paymaster, as if you couldn't guess, was none other than Mr. Brown. The wives must have sworn him to secrecy because he never told any of us what our wives were doing.

Gretchen later told me that all of the wives pilfered the same amount each month. That way, if the husbands ever did discuss their pay, the amounts for each would be the same. The balance of the pay was sealed inside an envelope and left on the kitchen table for the husband to find and open. What makes this story even more novel is that when I opened my envelope, I always took out ten dollars and stashed it inside one of my boots. I was going to use the money to help Gretchen furnish her farmhouse. I never found out about Gretchen's conspiracy until she told me the day my contract ended. I shared my secret that same day. We were both overjoyed.

"With what my parents had in savings coupled with what they saved during the five years on the railroad, they had a significant bank account. Besides their 'friendly embezzlement,' they became creative in other areas. Dad told me that two of the women owned sewing machines, and those machines were constantly in use making clothing and household extras out of whatever material the women could find. It looked like my parents were going to be in great shape and finally break the Stanford poverty string," Bill said.

We pooled our food, and on most Saturday evenings, everyone would dump vegetables and meats into a community stew pot. Out would come the benches and tables, and in the cool evening breeze, we would eat together under the stars. Singing and dancing usually followed the meal. Naturally, Lars provided the accompaniment. It was one gigantic picnic, and we all looked forward to it, but the children talked about it all week.

Our food allowance was sufficient to cover the costs of our food with enough left over to cover most gifts and some entertainment. Our only "splurge" was if we went on a weekend vacation.

Our wives were certainly ambitious and hard working. The two sewing machines were in constant use and while some of the women busied themselves making fresh bread, others were tending children—generally Tina Bedford—or doing the community laundry. Gretchen was skilled with a paintbrush, and she and a few of the other women started to whitewash all of the cabooses. Mr. Brown provided the paint and took it out of his store maintenance budget. The community town went from a dull gray to a shiny white within just a few days.

The women had something in common. They wanted the security that accompanied land ownership. They were going to be together for five long years and knew that they needed to live in harmony.

Bill added, "Dad made an entry relating to how the women decorated, landscaped, and beautified the community. He also wrote a little about the interaction between the community and the transient workers. Where dates have significance, I will add them."

One of the railroad agents found a hundred pound sack of abandoned wildflower seeds on a freight car. He carried it to the community and placed it conspicuously on our front steps. Within hours, all of the ladies were out with shovels, rakes, hoes, and anything that would break up the hard soil. Within a few months, the community took on a new color with wildflowers surrounding the units.

Each morning, the women would scurry down to the loading dock and pick up wooden remnants of discarded or broken wooden shipping containers. One of the husbands was a carpenter, and one Sunday I worked with him, and we spent the entire day building window boxes and planters. The scraps of wood left over were then placed in the neighborhood fire box. Neither of us felt badly about missing church; we were doing such a noble thing for our wives, and the good deed kept us from having to pray in church.

Often, the dock would be crowded with transient workers waiting to go to work. The women pleasantly greeted the men, and often these men would assist them in their wood collection. Frowns and disdain for each other were eventually replaced with smiles and laughter. The whole town of Logo was becoming a more pleasant community. Even the engineers and their families started behaving like regular people.

There wasn't much to clean in the units after the beds were made, floors swept, dishes and clothes washed, so our good women devoted their extra time and energy toward making their surroundings blossom. A few of the women would take on the responsibility of babysitting while the rest worked in the yards and gardens.

We worked together and formed deep friendships.

One morning, Gretchen was surprised to find a large sack of wheat and a bag of potatoes in front of her door. At first she thought it came from Mr. Brown, but when he was asked, he denied any knowledge of it. She naturally shared the prize with her neighbors.

A few days later, several planks of lumber and some nails mysteriously appeared in front of our unit. There was enough lumber to construct a large sandbox for all of the kids. Our resident community carpenter worked all evening and had it finished by the next day. The railroad had no shortage of sand, and Mr. Brown loaned me a wheelbarrow so we could haul sand to fill the children's sandbox. We took turns pushing the wheelbarrow, and forty trips later, we had the box filled.

The gifts generally arrived after dark. Gretchen waited up late one night to try to identify the donors so she could express her gratitude, but that particular evening, no one came. Gretchen was simply too curious to let the generosity continue without knowing the identity of the benefactor.

Then late one Saturday evening, Gretchen heard some muffled voices coming from our backyard. She didn't wake me, but when she peered through the curtains, in the moonlight she got a glimpse of their benefactors.

The noise was coming from about a dozen men whom she immediately recognized as part of the transient crew. They were assembling children's playground equipment next to the sandbox. Well, our ideas about the hardened, uncouth, unfriendly transient workers instantly vanished. These men had seen a way to help us and had used their free time to construct swings, slides, teeter-totters, and climbing bars. Some of them probably had children, and by helping us, they were helping themselves feel better.

The construction work was probably done inside one of the helper sheds. The playground set was huge and must have taken them weeks to build before they relocated it to our community. To make it even more personal, each of the large support logs contained carvings of smiling faces. It was a child's dream with a dozen totem poles support columns.

By midmorning, Gretchen had let everyone in the community know who had been showering us with gifts.

The transients had seen how hard the women worked, and they anonymously contributed items that they thought would make life easier for us. They were all too proud to accept thanks, so what they did, they did in the dead of night.

A few days later, we men all left for work. Apparently, as soon as we were out of sight, the women spent most of the day baking cakes, pies, and cookies. They made punch, and shortly after we returned home, they loaded us up with food and drink. We were directed to accompany them to the bunkhouse of the transients.

We were all worried about this venture, but we knew better than to challenge a bunch of determined women who had already cemented their intentions in their minds. Gretchen assigned me the task of knocking on the door and inviting the workers to come outside.

The men were a little embarrassed that their secret was out, but the gesture of friendship and the warmth of the women had touched their hearts. It took a few minutes before the workers slowly and reluctantly came out of the building, but soon the two groups mingled, laughed, and ate until it was the children's bedtime. Many of the workers played with the children and held them on their shoulders as they pranced around the yard.

From that day forward, there were seldom any obscene comments, off-color jokes, or rudeness shown in front of any of us. Doors were opened for the women. The transients used their free time to carve whistles and stick horses that they gladly gave to the young children. Mr. Brown's candy counter continually had to be restocked.

Gifts were now openly given consisting of food, candy, fruits, and one day, a huge smoked ham. No one even tried to guess where the ham came from. We were now indeed a community of harmony and love.

Something else was new. Occasionally, a few of the transients came to church and stood in the back of the room. They didn't own "Sunday best" clothing, so they came dressed in their cleanest coveralls. None of them would ever take a seat even though one was offered.

Each day the children play in the sand or on their new playground equipment and little Tina Bedford supervises their activities and plays with each of them as if they were all the same age. The children all idolize Tina, and often they will come to her caboose and ask if she can come out to play. As far as they were concerned, Tina was their same age, and seldom did she ever refuse.

In her free time, Tina has fashioned a vest for each child. The boys wore blue, and the girls wore pink. Every child had a vest, even the infants in arms. The pride shows in their faces as they adorned themselves in matching vests and climbed, jumped, and competed. Tina is everyone's favorite person, and she is always happy and full of fun and has many ideas for things for the children to do.

September 17, 1921 (Sunday)

Logo finally got a minister. He went by the name of Preacher Ox. He won't tell us his given name, so we just call him Preacher. He is a short, rotund man weighing well over three hundred pounds. A thick-pointed beard covers his chin—the rest of his face is clean-shaven. Gretchen thinks that he looks like Friar Tuck. His Bible was always in his left hand. I think he even slept with it. He hailed from Salt Lake City and made visits to various small towns along the rail line. Logo was his most easterly stop, so we held services closer to noon rather than in the morning. He would show up on the train in Logo at precisely twelve o'clock, and services would begin five minutes later. The train whistle would sound three short blasts when the preacher arrived.

Musical accompaniment was added. Lars borrowed a spare hymnal from Seth, and over a period of a few weeks, he memorized about ten hymns suitable for church. "Rock of Ages" played on a banjo added a little more gusto than when played on a piano or organ. The music added to the meeting and kept most of the congregation on key and singing together. Between Lars's banjo and Preacher Ox's loud voice, no one sleeps though one of his meetings.

"For a period of time, Dad didn't write anything in his journal. It was obvious when he did write that some dullness and boredom had settled into his life."

January 30, 1922 (Monday)

For me, the days now are virtually all the same. My very first job was to load, unload, and drive a wagon. It appears that job is now my lot in life and has become my permanent function. On rare occasions, I am called upon to work with pick and shovel, but that work is only temporary. I am blessed to have the job, but it would be nice to have some variety.

I continue to get up at six o'clock, and I am on the loading dock by seven. I now travel a half an hour because the railhead has moved southward several miles. It is now bitterly cold, so we all wear heavy coats, shirts, and pants.

Even though I get paid for a ten-hour day, I spend an hour of that time in transit and another half hour eating my noon meal. Union Pacific is a great company to work for, and I shouldn't ever feel discouraged about anything.

I can think back just a few years when I worked thirteen hours a day for twenty-five cents an hour. I will be happy to see the warmth of spring return.

Lars still strums his banjo to and from work and now during the soft-labor time before we come home. Mr. Pyle looks at Lars as being the musical doctor for the group. I don't know how he can keep playing when his hands get so cold. I guess he is still used to the weather in Norway. He hasn't memorized many Christmas tunes, but Norwegian folk music sounds good anytime.

The worst part is that we feel sorry for our wives when we have to be away from them sixty hours a week. We don't get time off for holidays, but we do very much enjoy getting our monthly Saturday to use as vacation and recuperation time.

March 7, 1922 (Tuesday)
When I awoke this morning, I found Gretchen on her knees in the bathroom clutching her stomach and throwing up. I was alarmed and raced to her side. She gently pushed me away and said she would be out in a minute.

When she finally came out of the bathroom, I was concerned and asked her if she was okay. I put my arm around her waist and kissed her cheek. She took me by my hand and led me into the bedroom. She patted the bed, and I sat down next to her.

"I don't want you to be alarmed, but you are going to be a father," she told me.

I was ecstatic and must have sounded rather stupid because I kept asking if she was sure. She kept saying yes. Finally, she grasped my face between her hands and spoke rather firmly to me. "I am sure, and Mrs. Brown thinks the baby will be born in September."

"In the second year of Dad's contract, I was born. I won't take the time to tell you about my younger years because I can't remember them. I can only tell you what my father told me about my early life.

"Apparently, my mother had a rather hard time while she was carrying me. Dad mentions several times in his journal about coming home and finding Mother sick in bed. She was often ill, and she had to force herself to eat. Often Dad fed her because she was too weak to feed herself. It was difficult for Dad to leave, but Mother was insistent that he go to work. She told him she would be fine.

"Dad was exceptionally healthy, and in the whole five years he never took a day off sick. He never missed his train or was late for work. He missed a total of four days of work in the full duration of his contract.

"The first day Dad was absent from work was the day I was born. It was on a Saturday morning, and as required by contract, he notified Mr. Brown. No pay was deducted, plus he got a congratulatory letter and a ten dollar bill from Mr. Stanford. The copy of that letter is pasted in the back of this book along with several others he received. Dad told me he couldn't have been happier. He spent the entire weekend helping Mom take care of me."

>October 5, 1922 (Thursday)
>Today, something new and miraculous happened. Early this morning, Gretchen delivered an eight-pound baby boy. We named him William after Gretchen's great-grandfather. She had a difficult time in labor, and had it not been for the patience and skill of Mr. and Mrs. Brown, we might have lost both her and our child. I have been sitting in a chair next to her bedside all night.
>Gretchen was so weak and so frail and was in labor for over nine hours. The community assisted and comforted us.
>Mr. Brown let Mr. Stanford know that I would not be in to work this morning.

October 8, 1922 (Sunday)
Gretchen is still so ill that she isn't able to nurse little William. Edith Egbert delivered a little girl three weeks ago, and for the present, she is wet-nursing both her child and William. Gretchen is so disappointed that she can't nurse her son but is so appreciative that Edith is willing and able. Gretchen realizes how time-consuming it is for Edith. Until Gretchen is well, she accepts what must be.

October 12, 1922 (Thursday)
When I got home from work this evening, little William was suckling at Gretchen's breast. She was absolutely overjoyed that she could finally care for her own infant son. Her radiance filled the room.

We both sat together and wept. William is a beautiful child. He had some bruises resulting from a difficult delivery, but they are fading, and he is looking much better.

I wish that Gretchen could put on some weight. She is still tiny and can hardly stand. Bertha Larsen fixes her meals and stays with her most of the day. Bertha currently has a seven-month-old boy of her own. The little tyke just sits on the floor and plays and coos. When I get home, Bertha leaves, and I take over.

November 6, 1922 (Monday)
It has been almost a month since William was born. He is growing by the hour. His color is good, and he grinned at me when I got home from work and picked him up. It may have been colic, but I like to think it was a little smile.

Gretchen is now up and around. She is slowly getting her strength back. Bertha still helps her a lot. We haven't had to fix a meal since William was born. Each evening, one of the neighbors brings over some type of casserole or meat loaf. If I keep eating like this, I will soon be as big as our preacher.

Bertha also keeps bringing over Norwegian concoctions that she wants Gretchen to drink. Apparently, Bertha feels that it adds nourishment to Gretchen's milk. I don't know about William, but Gretchen is getting her good color back. Bertha has some potion for almost any ailment. Maybe that is why I have stayed so healthy. Come to think about it, I have never seen any of the Larsen family ill.

Bill added, "Apparently, my mother did recover most of her strength. It took several months, but by early May, Mom was out in the yard and garden with the rest of the neighbors."

August 10, 1923 (Friday)
This is the second time that I have missed work. It is the first death of anyone in our group, and it is especially sad. Our precious little Tina gave birth to a little girl six months ago. Tina had just turned eighteen, and everyone in the community threw her a birthday party. Her caboose was decorated with ribbons, balloons, and confetti. There was cake, ice cream, and a lot of singing. She was still in her teens with two children under the age of two.

Today, Tina, Gretchen, and two other women volunteered to gather wood chips for the stoves. Bertha had given birth a month earlier to her second child. She insisted that she could tend both of Tina's children and William while Tina and Gretchen helped collect kindling. It would only be for an hour, and she would be fine.

The four women collected kindling, piled them, and wrapped and tied the wood into bundles and headed toward home. Tina spotted another piece of broken wood protruding between railroad ties. She put her bundle on the ground, and while on her knees, she stretched to retrieve the large protruding splinter. She was told to forget it, that they had enough kindling, but while still reaching, Tina turned her head and laughingly shouted to them, "Waste not, want not."

They all heard the buzz at exactly the same time as the immense diamondback rattlesnake struck. The fangs sunk into her neck just below Tina's right ear. Tina grabbed at the snake and pulled its head away from her neck. She then screamed and started to run toward her caboose. The women ran after her and made her sit while they quietly reassured her. One woman crushed the snake with a large rock.

Mr. Brown heard the scream and raced the hundred feet to where the women were located. He carried Tina into his bedroom and gently placed her on the bed. Seth immediately sent one of his sons to find Tina's husband and bring him back. An engineer aware of the problem volunteered the use of a helper engine.

Meanwhile, Mr. and Mrs. Brown worked frantically, but within just a few minutes, the poison had done its work. Tina was fading fast, and she wanted to hold her babies. Gretchen raced back to Bertha and quickly returned with Tina's two children in her arms.

Tina opened her eyes and smiled. She held a child in each arm and kissed their foreheads as tears streamed down her cheeks. Slowly, she tilted her head, first to the one child and then to the other. With the smile still on her face, she died. Even in death, she wouldn't release her protective grip. Her hands had to be pried from their bodies.

Jake was notified, but none of the men knew the seriousness of the wound. Our foreman, Mr. Pyle, asked me to accompany Jake. I did my best to console him and assure him that snakebites normally didn't kill a person, just made them ill. I sat with him as we both said a prayer—she would be fine. The return trip was completed within ten minutes. Never had a helper engine made that trip so quickly.

We thanked the men for their help as we raced into the store. Seth met us at the door. Mrs. Brown supported Jake as she led him into the bedroom where Tina's body lay. Jake bent over his wife and openly wept. He patted her cheek, kissed her gently, and then retrieved his children from Gretchen. He sat on a chair next to his wife and held his children close to him. We left him alone to be with his family. He stayed in the Brown's bedroom for nearly an hour. We could all hear him softly sobbing and gently talking to Tina and to his children, making promises.

August 13, 1923 (Monday)
The funeral was held in the meeting room today after work. Two of us built a casket yesterday that will house Tina's tiny body. We asked for, and UP granted, permission to bury her under a shade tree on the edge of the property. It was the first burial in the new Logo cemetery. Preacher Ox made a special trip to handle the services and dedicate the grave. The preacher opened the services with a beautiful prayer and then dedicated the grave site. Both of our foremen, Sherwood Pyle and Jon Ernstrom, attended the funeral and were supportive to Jake.

There were two speakers besides the reverend. Seth and I both offered some words of encouragement to the family and honored the life of Tina Bedford. All eleven of the caboose community wives sang hymns. The thought was certainly a fine one, but not one of them could control their tears. At the end of the service, several of us handed the preacher some money that he gratefully accepted. Jake was not required to go to work until such time as he felt up to it.

Jake had two children to care for, and that is when the community really banded together. Bertha insisted that she care for the children and admonished Jake to keep working.

"You'll need a farm, and we can care for the children until your contract is over. By then the little boy will be almost five, and the little girl will be three. We can't replace Tina, and we won't try. I am a big woman, and my milk will be sufficient to feed my baby and yours, and it is something I want to do. Something I need to do," Bertha said.

Jake recognized the wisdom of this amazing woman, and he gratefully agreed. On Monday Jake was back on the job. Lars and I kept him close. I was given Friday and Saturday off with pay so I could stay close to Jake. I later received a thank-you letter from Mr. Stanford.

September 7 1923 (Friday)
I have now worked for the railroad over two years, and today a rather sad, but not life threatening thing happened, and I want to record it in my journal.

This Friday morning, Lars, Jake, and I were unloading rails from a flatbed car. We were doing fine, just the three of us, but the foreman decided that it would be a good experience for a new man to help us. The gangly young fellow was unfamiliar with the lifting procedure. We tried to explain how we operated, but he figured he knew it all.

"It doesn't take that many brains to unload a flatbed," the man said. "Let's just get it done."

Before we were ready and without any warning, he lifted one end, but he didn't realize how much it weighed. He let the heavy steel rail drop, and it landed sideways and sliced off the end joint of Lars's little finger on his right hand. The rail cut it off as clean as if it had been done with a sharp knife.

Lars's English had improved considerably over the years, but it was probably good he didn't know any English cuss words, or he would have had one strike against him. He jumped off the train in obvious pain and loudly shouted something in Norwegian to the young man. The line boss raised his eyes and turned his head away. There was a slight smile on his face. He didn't know what Lars had said, but he chose to ignore the outburst. Even Mr. Stanford might have approved of the choice words Lars used under the circumstances.

Of course, the offender was very sorry, but that made no difference to the line boss or to Lars. The man was fired on the spot.

There wasn't much anyone could do with the missing finger, so it was retrieved and wrapped into a handkerchief and stuffed into Lars's shirt pocket. The bleeding was cauterized with a red-hot knife blade. Lars bit into his leather belt while the searing procedure was being performed. With his hand wrapped in bandages, he was sent back to Logo to get additional help. Mrs. Brown is a trained nurse, and we hoped that she could repair some of the damage.

Lars and I traveled back to Logo sitting in the warmth of the engineer's cabin. The recently unemployed culprit rode alone on the flatbed.

Lars clutched his banjo in his left hand on the ride to Logo. We were all very concerned for Lars's welfare and how his inability to do the same type work for a while would impact his contract, but we were also selfishly worrying about his ability to play the much-enjoyed banjo.

When we returned to Logo, the young man was immediately dispatched to one of the temporary flophouses while waiting for his ride to Ogden. He was instructed to stay inside and speak to no one for fear that somebody might strangle him.

I assisted Lars from the train, and the two of us walked in to see what could be done about Lars's finger.

Without fanfare, Mrs. Brown removed the old bandage and carefully examined the wound. Lars flinched each time the finger was touched—the burnt flesh hurt more than the cut.

Mrs. Brown rolled and handed him a clean handkerchief. "Bite down and try not to be a sissy," Mrs. Brown admonished.

Without further words, she tightly gripped his hand and began washing away soot and dry blood. She poured iodine on the wound, and Lars's eyes widened as he jumped up and down and bit hard into the cloth. If looks could have killed, the gaze that he gave Mrs. Brown would surely have taken her life. She ignored the look and continued to scrape away dead, burnt skin before suturing the wound. She poured on more iodine and then wrapped his finger with a roll of gauze. The sweat poured from Lars's forehead. When she was through, she grasped his head between her pudgy hands and gave him a kiss on the forehead.

"There, it will be almost as good as new," she said.

I was grateful that Lars didn't know where to find the young man that had caused him the injury. Sore finger or not, he would have most certainly strangled him. Lars was wobbly, so I helped him back to his caboose. Bertha didn't learn about the accident until after he returned from work, but when he walked in, she was very sympathetic and did a lot of coddling. She mixed up a batch of her cure-anything medicine and made him drink every drop. Frankly, I wouldn't have been surprised to see the finger grow back!

September 9, 1923 (Sunday)

Bertha delivered a plump baby boy this morning. This happened just two days after Lars's injury. Naturally, the attending medical people were again the Browns. No pay was deducted, and Mr. Stanford sent a congratulatory letter and ten dollars. Lars was given two days off with pay to help his wife with the new baby and to let his finger heal better.

September 10, 1923 (Monday)

Lars simply wouldn't stay home. Last evening Bertha cut off the fabric from the end of his glove so that his swollen and bandaged finger would fit, and bright and early, Lars was back to work today. Several allowances are being made for him until his finger is healed. Not once did he complain or use his injured hand as an excuse for not working hard. I still wonder what Bertha's reaction was when she washed Lars's shirt and found the end of his finger in the wash water.

"Dad told me that Lars didn't give up playing his banjo, and each evening he picked away until he could play it without using the pinky finger on his right hand. Occasionally, a funny note would come forth, but by the time the contract ended, he was as good as ever."

> Over the life of the contract, twenty-three children were added to the population of the small community. Two newborns died and are buried under the shade of the elm tree next to Tina. She would know how to care for them.
> As the years went on, the men naturally got older and wearier, but the love they received from their wives and families kept them going. The women all knew how hard the men worked and they knew better than to complain about how tough their days had been. They were greeted with hugs, smiles, and warm food, and miraculously, the stiff muscles, blisters, and aching backs were quickly forgotten. They wondered if Mrs. Stanford had given them a pep talk like Mr. Stanford had done to the men.
>
> October 20, 1923 (Saturday)
> Occasionally, the rigors of the long week get to some of us. It isn't really significant, but I want to make note of it. We openly talk about whether or not it is worth our time and effort. At those times we share words of encouragement and once again realize how important our goal of land ownership is. I am pretty sure we can get through these hard times. We all have the same goals and are working for the same end results. Thankfully, none of us were down at the same time, or we might all have quit!

"Dad told me that he and Mom lived in the community for the full five years. Each of the men who had signed the contract fulfilled the terms fully.

"Dad mentioned that Jake was a survivor. He told me that he met Jake several years later when he made a trip to Pocatello. Jake had remarried and owned six hundred acres of irrigated land. He and his new wife were actively involved in raising sugar beets and more children."

November 20, 1925 (Friday)
Great news awaited me when I got home from work this evening. Gretchen informed me that she was again with child. This time I didn't ask if she was sure. She figured the baby would be born in June, and it was obvious she was happy.

"The baby would be born after the railway contract ends. We will have our own farm by then," she assured me.

If it is a boy, we are going to name him Michael. If it is a girl, then we will name her Mary after my mother. Frankly, I hope it is another boy so William can have a baby brother, but more importantly, I hope that Gretchen is strong enough to have another baby.

December 18, 1925
We are only five months away from completing our railroad contract. It should be a happy time, with Christmas not far away. But today was a horrible day.

Our regular foreman didn't come to work again. He has been ill for three days. Mr. Stanford told him to stay home until he got well.

To take Mr. Stanford's place, a substitute foreman was dispatched from Ogden. Furthermore, Leonard doesn't know what he is doing, so compensates for his lack of ability by shouting orders. He refuses to listen to suggestions or recommendations from the crew.

The first thing he did was to order us to put 120 ties on each wagon. That is twenty more ties than we normally haul, and the added weight could cause damage to both the horses and the wagons. We had been loading wagons for four and a half years without any major problems. We had occasionally broken axles, but that was considered to be normal wear and tear because of the craggy terrain. I was the lead man, so I spoke up to recommend that we carry the normal load. Leonard became livid and threatened to fire me on the spot if I challenged one more of his orders. He criticized Sherwood, our regular foreman, for making short loads, which was costing the railroad extra money. I backed off, but in hindsight, I probably shouldn't have. I had nothing more to say. He actually frightened me. What if he did have the authority to terminate me with only six months left on my contract?

Everyone in our crew heard his rampage, but we were all too dumbfounded and frightened to do anything but follow his instructions.

The skinners had been observing Leonard's new loading procedure, and they were becoming more irritated by the minute. When it finally came time to hitch up the horses, the skinners were livid.

Lars is still sitting shotgun with me on the wagon. His English is much better, and I have no trouble understanding him. We were in and had just finished loading the last tie. One angry skinner headed toward me carrying an ax handle. Lars saw him storming toward me. I was about to get clumped good when Lars intervened. Lars being a big man grabbed the skinner from behind and lifted him off the ground. The man's arms were clamped to his side, and his feet were in the air. He struggled, kicked, and gasped for air. The skinner finally released his grip on the ax handle, and it dropped to the ground. Lars let the man go, and he crumpled into a heap at Lars feet.

"Youse is going ofder de wrong man, you are. Vee is yoost following de bosses orders. Now yoos go back and tend to yur animals," Lars told him.

Another skinner appeared, one far more rational than the man slumped on the ground. "Why are you overloading the wagons? The extra weight could kill our animals." He frowned with concern.

I told him that it wasn't my idea, and that when I complained, I had been threatened with my job. I said that the wagons are also more likely to be damaged and that we still have to unload, but now we have to haul sixteen additional ties to a different stacking location. That would mess up our return schedule.

The skinner reluctantly hitched up the team.

"I need to speak to Mr. Stanford about this," the skinner said.

Fifteen minutes later, the animals were heaving and pulling the much-too-heavy loads.

It wasn't until later that I learned that our third wagon only got about a half mile from the rail flatbed when an axle broke. Replacing an axle is something we have all done dozens of times, but it is never easy. The wagon must be unloaded, the axle replaced, and then reloaded. It is time-consuming and strenuous work.

The first two wagons were way ahead of him, so we in front didn't know he had a problem. The two men stopped the wagon, but in their haste to angrily unload the ties and get back on schedule, they forgot the cardinal rule that says the driver must stay on the wagon while the loader hobbles the horses. Anyway, something spooked the animals, and they bolted. The wagon still contained over seventy ties, and when the horses ran, the ties started falling. One wheel fell off, but the frightened horses kept running and dragging its cargo. The wagon eventually hit a rut and tipped over. There was nothing left of the wagon, it was totally destroyed. Even worse than the loss of the wagon, was the loss of a valuable horse. The wagon tongue had tangled with the legs of the animal, and both rear legs were broken. The horse would have to be destroyed.

After hearing about the problem, the track foreman raced to our location to let us know what had happened. He instructed us to dump our load and go help the other workers pick up the scattered ties.

It was a horrible mess. The wagon was busted, a horse was in agony, and ties were scattered over a quarter-mile area.

The skinners were immediately notified, and they hitched up an empty wagon with two fresh horses.

The track foreman dispatched most of his work crew to help pick up the ties, and it took us about forty minutes before the ties were reloaded. At about the time we returned to the injured horse, the angry mule skinners appeared. One man knelt by his beloved horse, stroked the animal's head, and wept.

None of the men carried a pistol, so the mule skinner stood above his horse and used a rail mallet to dispose of the animal. It took but one blow to the back of its head. Ropes were tied around the animal's neck, and then a dozen or so men hoisted it onto the skinner's wagon. There were a lot of angry looks, but none of the skinners became violent.

"It's cold. You have all worked way too hard today. Let's call it a day," the track foreman told us.

December 22, 1925 (Tuesday)

The railhead is nearing Salt Lake City and our ride to and from Logo is a lot longer now. It takes us an hour each way. UP has cut our lunch period down to twenty minutes. None of us feel badly, the company has been exceptionally good with us.

Seth Brown brought in a medical doctor from Salt Lake to look at Gretchen. The doctor was already gone when I got home, but Seth told me what he found out. Apparently, Gretchen has some type of intestinal blockage that isn't letting her digest her food. The doctor did a lot of pushing and prodding and then gave her some medicine. She doesn't look better even though she tells me she feels fine.

December 23, 1925 (Wednesday)

Gretchen is actually feeling a little better this morning. I browned some bread on the stove and then fed her oatmeal and toast. She was able to eat the hard food and actually asked for a second glass of milk. I sure hope that the doctor finds her problem and is able to correct it.

When we got to our workstation, thankfully, our track boss was back. He still looked bedraggled, but apparently, the skinner got hold of Mr. Stanford, and his story prompted his return.

The foreman wouldn't provide us with details, but apparently, the temporary foreman wasn't fired, but a portion of his salary was deducted each month to pay for the horse, wagon, and a portion of lost labor time because of his error in judgment. He was reassigned to a labor crew working with a pick and shovel. I doubt we will ever see him again.

When I got home this evening, Gretchen said that she is feeling much better. She was able to keep down her food, and that is a good sign. She takes her medicine, even though she says it tastes terrible.

December 25, 1925 (Friday)
Today we all got Christmas off, and Gretchen insisted that we go to church even though it wasn't Sunday. I reluctantly agreed.

Our gifts were few, and what money we did spend was on small inexpensive toys for William—things he can use in the sandbox. Gretchen fixed up a roast chicken with mashed potatoes and gravy. She is proficient now at baking bread.

Gretchen tired quickly, so much of the day was spent with her resting on the bed while I read her some Christmas stories.

January 4, 1926 (Monday)
Gretchen overworked fixing Christmas dinner, and that exaggerated other problems with her pregnancy. Bertha Larsen helps her during the day while I am gone, and even though she has a family of her own to care for, she is so full of goodness, she simply won't say no.

This evening Bertha brought over some meat loaf and baked potatoes. It tasted good, and William couldn't seem to get enough. Gretchen nibbled and got down half of her serving. When I am around, I make her drink a lot of fluids so she doesn't get dehydrated.

May 9, 1926 (Saturday)
Today was the day we have all been waiting for. My contract says I won't be finished until May 10, but since that is Sunday, this will be my final day with Union Pacific.

We assembled on the platform ready to go to work but were unexpectedly met by Mr. Stanford, a group of photographers, and reporters. To our surprise and delight, Mr. Stanford gave us the day off and then made a few comments.

"Union Pacific is proud of what you men have accomplished, and we want the rest of the world to know."

The photographers took our pictures, and the reporters asked us questions.

Bill interjected. "Dad told me that on the final day of his contract, the railroad grade had been completed north to Pocatello and South to Salt Lake City, and the lines were within sight of both cities."

We were overjoyed and had no apprehension about shouting UP's praises. Both the line and rail foremen were on hand to laugh with us and loudly recalled embarrassing experiences relating to our misadventures. Railroad officials and engineers stopped by to shake our hands and wish us well. There were reporters from local and national newspapers. I even gave an interview to a newspaper reporter from Denver, Colorado. You can be sure that I was full of compliments, but that was easy. It was because of Union Pacific that I now faced a future of something other than poverty.

Our railroad working days were over, unless of course we elected to reenlist, but we were all basically farmers at heart. We were ready to lay down seed rather than track.

This evening we hauled out the tables, benches, and chairs into our communal city center courtyard. We consolidated every scrap of food we had left in camp. We invited the engineers and their families, the transients, and everyone who would be willing to attend. They all came. Mr. Brown locked up his store, probably for the first time in years, and even supplied a whole pig and a side of beef. The butchered animals were placed on spits and slow-roasted over wood coals. It was a feast to remember. The railroad executives and most of the reporters stayed in Logo the full day, and they showed up at the dinner too. Suited men and workers in coveralls sat together and ate dinner.

The transients huddled together, and after the festivities ended, they inconspicuously drifted away. Gretchen and Bertha detained them long enough to load them up with food.

"We can't eat it all this evening, and we will be leaving early in the morning. If you don't take it with you, then it will go to waste," Bertha told them.

Her argument was persuasive, and the men happily bundled up the food. These men didn't get a food allowance, so this was a stroke of good fortune for them.

At the end of the meal, which incidentally lasted three hours, Mr. Stanford stood and asked the group for permission to speak. He reintroduced the executive, and then turned the time over to Bentley Cox, vice president of Union Pacific.

Mr. Cox delivered his speech, and we all listened intently. There were dozens of questions we wanted to ask, but we patiently held our tongues.

"I have been instructed to tell you all something. This program was initiated five years ago, as you all know. There were twenty-eight workers who signed the land-credit contract. It was a successful program, and the president of Union Pacific wanted me to personally convey that information to you. What you don't know is that of that original group, only sixteen workers fulfilled the full term of the contract. Twelve of you are seated here this evening."

There were loud cheers and applause. Mr. Stanford stood and applauded even more loudly than the workers.

"You have worked hard, through rain, snow, blazing sun, and scouring winds, but you made it, and you have made Union Pacific proud—you are to be commended. You good women have had to put up with many of the same discomforts, but you have come through it all and are better people because of it, I am sure. Mr. Stanford has indicated that some of you have lost family members while living here, and I express my condolences and remorse."

I looked at Jake as he held his two children next to him. He looked proud, but a tear stained his cheek.

Mr. Stanford concluded by letting us know that the railway between Pocatello and Salt Lake City was only two months from being completed and would be done on time and within budget.

The executive then opened a briefcase and took out a stack of envelopes. "I am about to call out names of the workers, and I will give each of you an envelope. Please do not open it until we are through with the presentation. Step forward when your name is called, and allow Mr. Stanford and me the honor of presenting it to you and the privilege of shaking your hands."

Our names were read, and in turn, we each stepped forward, shook the men's hands, and took the envelope. When all of us were through with the formality, the UP executive spoke again. "Inside the envelope, each of you will find what you were promised five long years ago: the title to your respective parcel of land."

Cheers and applause again sounded throughout the camp and filled the night air.

"It has been duly recorded, and all you will have to do is sign the necessary paperwork in front of a notary in your respective county courthouses. You will also find a first-class train pass. It is good for five years and will allow you and members of your family to ride anywhere in the Union Pacific's system."

Again, cheers and applause filled the night air.

"Stay with us for another fifteen years, and we will give you a lifetime pass," Mr. Cox said.

Mr. Stanford held up his hand for us to quiet, and the suited man continued. "You will also find an envelope, which contains a congratulatory letter from Mr. Stanford and from the president of Union Pacific. They thank each of you and commend you for your efforts. What you have accomplished is no small feat, and you will be able to point to this two-hundred-mile stretch of track with pride. Your children and grandchildren will share that pride. Don't throw that envelope away because inside it you will find something else. You may now open your envelopes."

After I opened my envelope, Gretchen took it from me before I could even read it. She was making sure I wouldn't misplace it.

Gretchen assured me that everything was there like the man said. Then her eyes got as big as saucers. She opened the small sealed envelope, and along with the letter from the president of UP, she held up five brand-new one hundred dollar bills and handed them to me. The air exploded with shouts and laughter. The crisp new bills were held high in the air. This was the first time in my life I had ever even seen one. Gretchen quickly took the bills back from me and clutched them next to her breast.

"Consider it a bonus of one-hundred dollars per year for five years of outstanding work and sacrifice. Union Pacific thanks you for your perseverance and dedication."

We raced forward and warmly thanked the UP executives. We walked with them back to the station and stood together on the platform for a full hour before their train arrived. We wanted these men to know how much we respected them and how much happiness they had brought into the lives of twelve families. The conversation was easy and comfortable. Formalities of employee-employer relationships were dispensed. For a time, we were all equals.

This has been a pretty good day for all of us.

We returned to our community, but no one could have possibly gone to sleep, with the exception of some of the younger children. Ovations kept breaking out. The party went on most of the evening, but eventually, people eased away from the bonfire and went to bed.

May 10, 1926 (Sunday)

We knew that the train taking us to Ogden wouldn't depart until two o'clock, so we had plenty of time to relax. Gretchen had already cleaned the caboose. We sat at the kitchen table and shared one orange, the remaining food item in our pantry.

A few minutes passed, and then Gretchen stood up and pulled down all of the blinds in our unit. She walked to the door and locked it, the first time it had been locked in the five years we had lived in Logo. I was puzzled, but soon my questions were answered.

Gretchen retrieved our Ogden bankbook and placed it in front of me at the table. To my amazement and delight, the account balance was nearly $8,000. Gretchen wasn't finished with her surprises. Bringing a pillow from our bedroom, she snipped a few stitches and retrieved a two-inch-high wad of bills. She grinned from ear to ear.

"There is $2,400 in that pile. I have saved forty dollars per month for our entire time in Logo," Gretchen proudly proclaimed.

I was overwhelmed. Not only was I surprised that she had saved so much from our monthly pay, but I was amazed that she had pilfered another forty dollars per month that I didn't even know about. I hugged her, and then with a sheepish grin, I unrolled one of my work socks and removed my stash. I put the $600 I had saved on the pile of currency.

I now knew why Gretchen nervously pulled down the shades and locked our caboose door. She wasn't about to get robbed on our last day in Logo.

"I can't believe that you were holding back money without telling me," she chastised.

We both burst into laughter.

Gretchen placed the five one hundred dollar bills onto the pile, and we started to add up the bounty.

"$11,509!" Gretchen shouted and then covered her mouth quickly and glanced around as if someone else was in the room.

We had enough money to buy a house and a barn. We could furnish the house, buy farm equipment, and put cash away for a rainy day. We were rich, rich, rich!

We stayed in our unit until almost noon. Gretchen sewed the money into the lining of her slip so tightly and with so many stitches that I knew it would take an hour in the bank to get the money into our account. Finally, we closed the door for the last time. We left the key in the door, picked up our luggage, and headed toward the station. William was walking fine, so he obediently walked beside us. Gretchen is pretty bulgy, so all she carried was the wicker picnic basket. We will never dispose of that item.

We were the next-to-last family to arrive at the station, and we were still two hours early. Mr. and Mrs. Brown came out of the store just moments after we arrived.

All trains went to Ogden, Utah, and from there the folks would be heading toward their newly acquired land. With the rail passes we had, we could have gone by way of San Francisco to get to our respective homes, but everyone was eager to get to their farms and start new lives.

Mr. Brown wanted to say something to us as a group. "We have been the store managers in Logo for many years, but these last five years have been our most enjoyable. We want all of you to know before you leave that we truly love and respect each of you. We have learned to know and love your children like they were our own. My wife and I have enjoyed our time with you, especially in our Sunday meetings. We will miss the musical accompaniment of our resident nine-fingered banjo player."

Lars Larsen and everyone else laughed.

"We have shared happy and sad times together, and you all will be truly missed," Mr. Brown continued. "We cannot let you leave without us doing one more thing. I recall when Samuel Spader promised that he would buy Gretchen a steak dinner from our diner. He never kept that promise. Today, my wife and I have prepared a steak feast for all of you. We want you to leave Logo with the taste of our good beef in your mouths. That should also satisfy Samuel's promise to Gretchen.

"Please don't say no. We want to do this thing. Take what time you need to eat. There is milk and other food for the children and for those who don't like steak.

"Don't worry about missing your train. I have already been assured that the train will wait, if necessary, to make sure you all get finished with your meal."

The families left their suitcases and other belongings on the loading dock and followed the Brown family into the diner.

"Dad told me that the food was delicious, probably the best meal he ever had. The Brown family would not accept a penny from any of the group.

"They hugged, kissed, cried, and exchanged mailing addresses. They further promised to never forget one another.

"I was three years old when we left Logo, so I don't really remember anything about that day, but Dad retold the story many times, I have no trouble picturing it," Bill said.

With our luggage stowed by the porters, we were saying our final good-byes before boarding. Suddenly from around the corner of the store came a group of probably sixty balloon-and-ribbon-waving people. The engineers, their families, and the transient workers showed up to bid us farewell. Everyone was waving and blowing kisses. The train was ready to leave, and our group didn't have time to talk. We waved, cried, and shouted farewells.

Sweat and Debt

"Dad made several journal entries about the time after he left Logo. He was anxious to get to his new farm," Bill noted.

After leaving Logo, we went to Ogden and from there caught another train to Cache Junction, Utah. It was the last train of the night, and the station agent agreed to use his own vehicle to haul our family and possessions the twenty-five miles to our farmland.

I brought with me a piece of canvas and a small tent, figuring that if we couldn't get a hotel room, we could sleep on the ground on our own land for one night. The evening was cool, but not cold. As we were spreading out the canvas under a large maple tree, a farmer in a nearby field saw us in the moonlight. Gauging from the rapid pace that he was moving toward us, it was evident that he was concerned that we were vagabonds or bums. He most likely was going to send us on our way.

When the man got nearer, we could see by his facial expression that he was upset. "My name is Alfred Pace, and you are on private land. I would suggest you pack up your gear and hightail it out of here!"

I surprised him when I extended my hand and introduced my family and then myself. Immediately, the man softened. I told him that I had been working for Union Pacific for the last five years to acquire this piece of property and received my deed a few days ago. I explained to Mr. Pace that I ultimately planned to build a house, barn, and get some seed into Mother Earth, but my most pressing need right now was to find a place to house my family.

I volunteered that I had saved some of my railroad pay (I didn't tell him how much), so I wasn't a vagrant.

Mr. Pace listened intently and occasionally nodded his head. He explained that we wouldn't be able to find a house to rent in the immediate area and noted that the nearest hotel was in Preston, Idaho, some twenty miles away.

"I own the property north and west of yours. I am thinking that you three will need a place to stay while your home and barn are being built. Maybe we can do each other a favor."

He had my full attention.

"Until two years ago, four Mexican families were living in those structures you see across the street. They were respectful and took good care of them. I hired them to help me during the picking season, but when it was over, they elected to move to California where the growing season was longer. I couldn't blame them for that. Anyway, they were good workers, and I hated to see them go.

"There were four units, but our tough winters have caused havoc on two of them. The others are still in pretty good condition. If you and the missus are willing to clean them up and maybe paint them, you can stay there until you find a place that suits you better. A place that is lived in lasts a lot longer than one that is vacant."

"Dad told me that my mother's eyes watered. She was so happy not to have to sleep on the ground with the bugs. A dry roof sounded like a palace to her. Dad could see how she felt, and his goal of sleeping on his own land the first night dimmed and died. Mr. Pace helped our family tote what few belongings we had about one hundred yards to the shacks. The huts were indeed in need of paint, and a few wallboards were missing, but they were habitable."

"You stay here as long as you want. If it's going to take a long time and if you are satisfied with living here, then you can have both shacks. How about five dollars a month rent for the two of them?" Mr. Pace asked.

"My father explained that he could afford to pay a higher rate and wasn't expecting charity, but Mr. Pace wouldn't relent."

"Five bucks a month is what I think they are worth. Take it or find another place. I hate to argue!"

"My father knew that it would be one or two years before the farm produced a salable crop, so he tearfully and graciously accepted Mr. Pace's offer of kindness. Dad told me that they stayed up a long time that evening, and as hard as they tried, they simply could not go to sleep. They kept talking about their good fortune," Bill said.

It was still dark outside when I was awakened by the sound of horses, voices, and machinery. I jumped from the cot and rushed to the door, rather disoriented. Peering out, I could see about fifteen men with horses and machinery. I quickly got dressed and walked across the road to where the men were standing in my field.

They shouted a friendly good morning and went on with their work. They didn't ask my opinion or seem to care what I wanted to plant. Shouting instructions to each other, they cranked up their metal-wheeled tractors and hitched plows to their horses.

Bill continued. "Dad told me that he worked alongside them all day, and one by one they introduced themselves. As hard as he taxed his memory, he simply couldn't remember all of their names. Each was dressed in overalls. Straw hats covered their heads and most of their faces. Their jackets were pulled up around their necks to protect them from the morning cool air, and most had beards. But the smiles on their faces he would remember for the rest of his life."

May 15, 1926 (Saturday)
At noon, everyone stopped and climbed into the back of a hay wagon. I headed back to the shack, but two men grabbed my arms and hustled me onto the wagon alongside the rest of the workers.

At a nearby farmhouse, several women had already set up tables and benches in the front yard. We reverently stood near the tables while Mr. Pace offered a prayer on the food.

Mrs. Pace came over with Gretchen and William. These amazing neighbors had gone to our shack and picked them up.

During the meal, the women came to introduce themselves. Gretchen and I tried to connect their names with their husbands, but it was just too hard to remember. It would take time, but we were dedicated to getting to know each of them.

We worked hard that afternoon and didn't quit until darkness finally stopped our progress. When the men called it a day, the field had been cleared of brush and weeds, plowed, and leveled.

"We'll be back first thing tomorrow morning, so you three get a good night's sleep!" one of the men shouted as he drove away.

I stood by the side of the road and waved at them as they left.

Gretchen and William met me at the door to our shack. She was excited about something. Grabbing me by the arm, she ushered me into the kitchen. There on the table were boxes of foodstuffs, and an icebox sat in the corner stuffed with milk, butter, meats, and cheese. The shelves were filled with bottles of fruits and vegetables.

More blankets and quilts adorned our bed, and a baby crib sat in our bedroom. Gretchen burst into tears when she showed me a small baby basket that Mrs. Pace had brought when she and four other women delivered the food. The wood box was full, and the stove was filled with wood and coal ready to light. We went to bed this evening content and grateful.

May 17, 1926 (Monday)
This morning, the same group that helped us on Friday was there but accompanied by even more men and horses. Several wagons stood next to the field loaded with farm tools and seed.

I asked the men what I had decided to plant this year. I didn't have the remotest idea.

Mr. Pace answered, "Well, Samuel, you have decided upon wheat. You made that decision because you knew you didn't have enough water to plant beets or corn. You also knew that you would make less money this year on wheat, but by next year you would have water from the new canal that you will be helping to dig. You also knew that you wanted to save what dollars you had so you could buy farm equipment and a horse."

All of the farmers were laughing.

"By spring next year, most of us will have a pretty good idea of what the consumers are going to need, and we'll oblige them. You just tag along for the ride until you get the knack of it.

"You were planning to help us dig a canal from the river to our farms. Don't you remember?"

"How could that have slipped my mind," I jokingly responded.

"We won't get it completed this year, but by fall of next year, it will be done, Lord willing. All you are going to need is a strong back and a weak mind. We will provide everything else," Mr. Pace said.

It was five o'clock when the work was finally completed. I now have eighty acres of farmland planted in wheat. There are irrigation ditches, and it is a beautiful sight to behold. Everyone who had worked on the field came over to the shack after we were finished. Gretchen had lemonade and cookies sitting on the edge of Mrs. Pace's wagon. All of the fixings came from Mrs. Pace, but she wouldn't take any credit.

I thanked all of my neighbors and asked the men how I could ever repay them. Mr. Pace answered for the group. "Just help the next person who comes along and is in need."

"My mother and dad stood next to me, and we all waved at the workers as they left. At least that's what my Dad told me I did."

July 10, 1926 (Saturday)
I was in the field irrigating when I suddenly had the worst feeling come over me. I had a premonition that I should go home and check on Gretchen and William. I didn't let the feeling pass. I shut off the water and raced to the shack.

When I got close to the door, I could hear William screaming at the top of his lungs. I thrust open the door and found Gretchen on the floor. She was pale, and she had foam at the side of her mouth. Her face was contorted, and she appeared to be in pain. She was rapidly flailing her left arm.

I carried her into the bedroom and placed her on the bed. It was urgent that I get help for her.

Carrying William under my arm, I sprinted toward Mr. Pace's farm. Fortunately, he was in his field. I shouted what had happened. He told me to go home and care for Gretchen. He would take care of everything else.

I ran back home still carrying William. The poor little boy had quit crying, but he looked terrified.

When I got to the house, I placed William on a stool close to me in our bedroom. I shut the door so he wouldn't wander away. Gretchen felt hot, so I rubbed her head and face with a wet towel. She was whimpering and writhing in pain. I was frantic. I didn't know what to do. I ran outside to see if Mr. Pace was coming, but he wasn't in sight. I went back into the bedroom and patted William on the head and then sat next to Gretchen. I asked her what I could do. I could barely see her through my tears. She clenched my hand so hard that her nails dug into my flesh. I didn't remove her hand until I heard the sound of horses, and then I bolted to the door. It was Mr. and Mrs. Pace, Dr. Hall, and his nurse.

The doctor pushed me aside without even speaking. He and his nurse raced into Gretchen's room. Little William was pushed into the kitchen, and the door was shut tightly.

I clutched William in my arms and held him close to me. His lips were quivering, and he was about ready to cry.

Mrs. Pace put her hand on my shoulder and tried to comfort me

A few minutes passed, and then the door flung open, and Dr. Hall came out of the bedroom carrying my tiny precious Gretchen in his arms.

"Get some blankets into my buggy, and do it fast," he told me.

Mrs. Pace took William from me, and I raced to get every blanket I could find.

The doctor gently placed Gretchen in the backseat of his buggy. She was crouched into a fetal position. His nurse jumped into the buggy next to the doctor and then swiveled so that she could care for Gretchen.

The horse was whipped, and the buggy raced onto the road. Dr. Hall shouted over his shoulder to me to let me know he was going to the hospital in Preston. I should get there the best way I could, but he couldn't wait for me. Mr. Pace and his wife encouraged me not to worry. The four of us got into their wagon. William and I sat in the back on a bed of straw.

Mr. Pace didn't spare the mare, and we rode as fast as she would go. Dust hung in the air from the doctor's wagon racing in front of us. When we reached the front entrance to the hospital, I jumped from the wagon and headed for the front door. Mr. Pace hitched the wagon and followed closely behind me. Mrs. Pace remained in the wagon with William. He was crying and had soiled himself. I glanced to see that she was tearing her petticoat to fashion him a diaper.

At the registration desk, I asked the receptionist where I could find my wife.

"Her name is Gretchen Spader, and Dr. Hall just brought her in."

The young woman was talking on the telephone about an upcoming wedding. She wrinkled her forehead and gave me a look of disgust. "I will be with you in a minute. Please sit down and be quiet." She continued with her conversation.

I became livid. Seldom in my life have I ever wanted to strangle a woman, but today my anger seethed over. I uttered a mild obscenity and leaped halfway over the counter in an attempt to grab the phone. Startled, the woman sprang from her chair, knocking it over in the process as she nervously backed away from me.

Just then, hands firmly grasp my upper arm. It was Dr. Hall. "Come with me."

He led me to a private office and asked me to please sit down. I remained standing and frantically explained that I needed to see Gretchen. He pointed to the chair and told me to sit down. The inflection in his voice left no doubt of his resolve, so I sat.

"Calm yourself. Gretchen has had a stroke. The right side of her body is paralyzed. I have given her enough medication to calm her, but it can't be stronger or it might be harmful to the baby. Gretchen is not in pain—probably never was. She was in fear of losing the baby and couldn't figure out what happened to her. Sometimes mental fear can be far worse than physical pain. Right now we are doing everything we can to relax her. I am going to let you see her, but you must be calm. I can't have you exciting her with your fear and anger."

I breathed deeply and assured him I would be calm. I washed my face in the basin and then walked into her room, the doctor right behind me.

I sat next to her bed. She covered the side of her face to shield it from me. I gently removed her hand and kissed her on the forehead.

"Now don't you worry! You are going to be fine. I brought William, but he is having so much fun with Mrs. Pace, I decided to let him play," I told her.

She attempted an awkward, wrinkled smile. She once again sobbed, but I touched her cheek with my hand and reassured her that she would be fine. I changed the subject several times, but I could not convince her that she would get well. She was self-conscious about her appearance.

Finally, the doctor reluctantly told me it was time to leave. "Gretchen needs some rest to get her strength and stamina back," he said.

I squeezed Gretchen's hand and kissed her gently on her lips.

Dr. Hall followed me into the foyer and told me to go home, that there was nothing I could do there. "Your little boy needs you, and I would rather have you home than here attacking my receptionists," he said.

For the first time all day, I mustered a laugh.

He told me that the unborn baby's heartbeat was still strong.

Mr. and Mrs. Pace took me home. William and I entered a lonely house, and for the first time in many years, I knelt at my bedside and asked God for help.

August 4, 1926 (Wednesday)

I have only been able to go to the hospital six times since Gretchen was admitted almost a month ago. I don't have transportation of my own, so I have to rely on the generosity of Mr. Pace. Mrs. Pace is always willing to tend William, and today Mr. Pace drove me to the hospital.

Gretchen has been having trouble breathing, and Dr. Hall is keeping her on oxygen day and night.

She is in a constant-care room, and a nurse remains by her side at all times. Dr. Hall has brought in two specialists from Salt Lake City, and both have worked extensively on her, but her paralysis isn't improving.

On my last visit a week ago, the administrator gave me a summary of the medical charges. I was overwhelmed. In just a little more than one month, the costs have exceeded $4,000, but I would gladly give everything I have to get my Gretchen home.

The ride home was long and difficult, and none of us spoke much about Gretchen or her condition.

When we got home, Mr. and Mrs. Pace told me that they wanted to walk home.

"We need the exercise, and besides, we would like you to keep the horse and wagon until you get Gretchen home again," Mr. Pace told me.

I am grateful to that man and woman. They are godsends.

August 7, 1926 (Saturday)

I took William with me to Preston. I have a hard time keeping interested in maintaining the farm while Gretchen is in the hospital. I need to figure out how to get her home so I can care for her here.

Dr. Hall wasn't on duty, but another doctor told me I could go in and see her. The desk receptionist offered to tend William while I was in her room.

She is so frail, and her face is pale. The nurse said that she was no longer eating enough to keep her alive. I sat by her bed and tried to feed her some custard, but she just shook her head and feebly brushed my hand away. She mustered a smile and then mumbled William's name.

I left the room and came back with William in my arms. I carried him over to her bed, but for an instant he was frightened.

The nurse was getting nervous. Children were not allowed, so she recited her rehearsed spiel about hospital rules, but my glare made her change her mind.

William didn't even know his mother. She covered the paralyzed portion of her face with her left hand. In that instant there was recognition, and William reached his tiny hands out to her.

I lay him next to her, and she held him close, keeping the droopy part of her face away from him. She couldn't turn her head far enough to look at him but kept stroking his head and rubbing her cheek gently against the side of his head.

I stayed for several minutes until Gretchen closed her eyes. William didn't fuss the entire time he rested on her arm. I gently removed him and let her sleep. I softly kissed her on her lips and stroked her silky hair.

The drive back was long. William is just learning to talk, and he kept repeating, "Mommy comes home?" His eyes look so sad.

In my own mind, I know the answer.

I tucked William in our bed and am now recording the events of this day. I am so lonely and tired, but I feel I must continue to document these events as they are happening. If nothing more than to someday let William know of his mother's love.

August 12, 1926 (Thursday)

It was still dark when a wagon drove up in front of the shack. I was already awake, and I lit a lamp and shuffled to the door. When I saw Dr. Hall's face, I knew.

I dreaded yet had expected this day.

He wrapped his arms around me, patted my shoulder, and whispered softly in my ear. "Gretchen went peacefully early this morning. We tried to save the baby, but the baby just wasn't strong enough. It was a little boy, and he died two hours later."

August 16, 1926 (Monday)

Dr. Hall and Mr. Pace handled all of the funeral arrangements. Many women offered to take William, but I refused. He was all I had, and we needed each other.

If the new baby was a boy, Gretchen and I had decided to name him Michael, so that is the name I carved on his wooden headstone.

"You were named after him," Bill said to his youngest son. "James, Grandpa Ezra's younger brother, purchased two plots in a new Pocatello cemetery, and he deeded one of the plots to Ezra and his posterity. Ezra and Nancy are already buried there next to Samuel, Gretchen, and Michael. Ruth and I have already agreed that our final resting place will be next to them."

August 17, 1926 (Tuesday)

I traded wheat for lumber and built two wooden caskets—one large and one small. On my wife's headstone I carved her name and the words "Rest in Peace, Beloved Wife and Mother."

I again borrowed the wagon from Mr. Pace, and he helped me load the caskets containing Gretchen and our little Michael. The ride took us four hours, and William never whimpered or made a fuss. I was sadly proud of him. He gave me added strength to make the journey.

Gretchen and I only lived together in those shacks for three months. We had worked so hard to achieve our dream, and it had vanished. She was only thirty-one years old.

The hospital and doctor's bills decimated over two-thirds of the money that we had saved, but I was determined to rebuild and make a life for little Bill and me.

"Dad lost interest in maintaining his journal and didn't make another entry for over two years," Bill added.

October 18, 1928 (Thursday)

Today I received two letters. One was from Uncle James and Aunt Lydia, and the other from my aunt Emma—my mother's sister.

I was rather happy to get two letters in the same day, but my happiness quickly faded to sorrow. My father and mother had both died of influenza on October 12. The letters arrived two days after they were buried. Ezra was sixty-three, and Nancy was fifty-nine.

I waited several minutes before I opened the letter from Aunt Emma. I was confident that it was going to tell me the same thing I had just learned. I was wrong. Her letter informed me that Mary Morgan, Gretchen's mother, had died in the same epidemic that took the lives of my parents.

October 19, 1928 (Friday)

Today I got six letters. Five of them were from people offering condolences at the loss of my parents.

The last letter I opened was a shock. It was another letter from my Uncle James and Aunt Lydia. They let me know that Gretchen's father, Benjamin Morgan, had frozen to death. James told me that after Mary died, he had tried to comfort Benjamin, but he was distraught.

Benjamin had lost both of the women he truly loved. It was so devastating to him that he lost his desire to live. James indicated that no one knew whether he went out into the woods and got lost accidentally or on purpose. Either way, he died leaning against a tree, holding a picture of his family in his hands.

I share in his sorrow and know his pain. In the past two years I had lost my wife, a child, my parents, and Gretchen's parents. I don't know how much more I can take.

All of my loved ones are buried in Pocatello, Idaho.

As soon as I regained my composure, I wrote letters to Uncle James and Aunt Lydia and to Aunt Emma. They needed to know how much I loved and appreciated them.

William just turned six on October 5, 1928. Each night since the death of his mother and grandparents, I have been telling or reading stories to him about them. I don't want him to forget, but he is so young. He will have to remember the stories I tell him, even if he doesn't remember them personally.

"All four of my grandparents were alive on my sixth birthday, but three weeks later they were all dead," Bill told his family.

"I recall the time that next January when my father got very ill. He couldn't get out of bed for over two months. I matured a lot in that time. I remember toasting bread on the top of the stove. I kept the house warm and fed Dad broth that Mrs. Pace brought to us. I learned how to heat soup and bake a potato. By the time he was well enough to get around, I was able to keep us both well-fed and warm. I had always hoped to save enough money to buy appropriate headstones and place them on my relatives' graves. I also want to visit with James and Lydia and thank them in person for all of their many kindnesses to me and my family," Bill vowed.

"You already know that I was born near here on October 5, 1922. After my mother died, my father never remarried. He raised me by himself. Most of the things I recall about my real early life came from stories that my father told me. I do remember most things that happened after I was about six.

"Father worked with the other farmers, and although it took two years to complete, the canal was finally delivering water. We had all the water needed to irrigate our entire farm.

"I accompanied Father wherever he went. While he dug out potatoes, I played in the dirt near him. When he ate, I ate, and when he slept, I slept. When he worked on the tractor, I sat next to him where I couldn't fall off. When he pitched hay, I did the same, but with a smaller wooden pitchfork that didn't have sharp points. We were inseparable.

"After Mother died, Father lost any interest in building a home. Most of the money we had was spent on farm equipment and seed. He did buy a used tractor, but it always was in need of repair. We occasionally took our wagon and rode the ten miles into Preston to pick up groceries, medicine, and clothing. Nothing was ever spent on frivolous things. We didn't own a car, a boat, or things like that. Father wasn't into sports, but he would occasionally come and watch me play baseball when I got older.

"We still lived in Mr. Pace's shack, but my father did a lot of remodeling and repair. He joined the two shacks together with a walkway and put in two more doors. He had to reroof both structures and extended the roofline to cover a long porch he built in front. All of the other shacks were dismantled, and much of the wood was used to construct the walkway. What scrap pieces remained were burned in the stove or used to form a wooden walkway from the road to the shack.

"We cleaned up all of the trash that had accumulated over the years, put it in a big pile, and had a bonfire. Father used his tractor to smooth out the area around the shacks and then got permission from Mr. Pace to plant some apple and pear trees.

"I didn't need to have anything bigger. This shack was a home just as long as I was with my father. We slept in one shack and used the other for cooking and parlor sitting. The parlor is where father would read to me. On warm evenings, we would sit outside on the porch, and he would tell me stories about my mother and grandparents or read me stories from the Bible or the classics.

"My father taught me a lot about farming and how to take care of the horses, the land, and myself. When I was about six, I was responsible for drying the dishes after Father washed them. I started school a year later, and my responsibilities expanded to cleaning the shacks, making the beds, and keeping coal and logs near the stoves. My father worked hard in the fields and in taking care of the horses. I just did what I could to make life a little easier for him, but each day he looked older, thinner, and more tired.

"I remember the first day I went to school. A neighbor stopped in front of our shack. I ran out and climbed into the back of a hay wagon and was hauled two miles to school. It was actually kind of fun to be able to ride and talk to the other kids. A woman teacher taught the younger children, whose ages ranged between six and ten. Children ages eleven through fourteen were taught by a man. A sheet that hung on a rope stretched down the center of the room separated the students. We could always hear the teacher instructing his students behind the sheet, but none of us had the slightest hint of what he was talking about.

"I had a few friends I met in school, but farm life was tough, and there simply wasn't time to form recreational friendships. I was in the eighth grade and in my class when a man in a dark-black suit tapped me on the shoulder and asked me to follow him."

"'I have some bad news,' the man said. 'Your father's tractor tipped over, and his legs and hips are busted up pretty bad. I am going to take you to the hospital to see him,' the man told me.

"We climbed into his buggy, and he raced to Preston without much conversation. When we got to the hospital, I was taken to my father's room. His legs were suspended high in the air and held by ropes, pulleys, and weights. Father's head was bandaged, and he was in a cast that went from his rib cage to his ankles. It was difficult to see my father in such bad shape. He mustered a smile when he saw me, but he was obviously in a lot of pain. He tried to comfort me that he would be okay. I sat next to his bed and held his hand for a long time. The man who brought me whispered that he had to leave. I thanked him, but I was so worried and distraught about my father, I forgot to ask him his name. Later when I was back in school, I inquired of my teachers and the principal regarding the identity of the man, but none of them remembered seeing a man in a dark-black suit. My teacher wasn't even aware that I had left the class.

"I was then, and still am, very puzzled by that event.

"Father remained in the hospital for over three months. I rode the horse to Preston every Sunday to see him, but the rest of my time was spent in school, doing homework, or working on the farm. There was a lot to do, and I had to get up early in the morning to get a head start. In the second month, I was getting behind in school and didn't have time enough to study or do homework. A lot of neighbors offered to help, but I just couldn't take advantage of them. They had work of their own. I did accept their gifts of food. I wasn't much of a cook, and roast beef was something I didn't know how to prepare.

"When I got home one Sunday, I made the decision that my formal schooling was over. From now on, I would have to school myself the best I could. When Father was finally discharged from the hospital, I borrowed Mr. Pace's hay wagon to bring him home. He lay on the straw surrounded by every blanket and pillow we owned.

"Father couldn't get out of bed without help, and he had to be on crutches just to go to the bathroom. I prepared his food and bathed him. He stayed in bed most days and couldn't sleep at night. He refused to take pain pills because they made him dizzy and he couldn't think straight. There was no way he could work on the farm.

"I was fifteen years old when I assumed full responsibility for plowing, planting, irrigating, and reaping along with the other duties required to keep the farm alive. Unfortunately, our equipment was wearing out at a rapid pace, and we didn't have the money to cover repairs or replacement. Our savings had gone down to less than two hundred dollars, and we had nothing of value to sell.

"It took eighteen months before Father was able to start working again. For the past year he had done all of the cooking, cleaning, laundry, and that type of work, but he simply wasn't strong enough to do heavy farmwork. Neighbors had suggested that Father sell the farm. Even though he knew it was the right thing to do, Dad and Mother had worked long and hard for too many years to lose it.

"I raised crops that didn't cost much for seed. This decision didn't make us much money, but it also didn't require much time or cash investment. I was seventeen when Father was finally able to do any significant chores around the farm. He couldn't yet lift, plow, or irrigate, but he could pitch hay and feed the horses. I couldn't handle the job alone of irrigating beets and corn, so I confined my farming to raising wheat.

"I was really grateful that we didn't have cows to milk twice a day. I barely had enough hours in a day to take care of the crops, let alone handle milking duties."

The War

"I turned nineteen in October of 1941, and in December, Pearl Harbor was attacked, and World War II began for America. I had expected to be drafted, so it didn't come as a surprise when, in February, I received my call to report for duty in the army. I could probably have gotten a deferment because I was an only son and also worked on a farm, but this was one call that I wasn't about to shirk. Father felt the same way, and he expressed his pride in me for making that decision.

"Our bank account had grown to around $600. and Father felt he could handle things on the farm by himself. He would have to take it slow, but his health had improved to where he felt he could manage.

"Father told me, 'You keep yourself safe, son. If things get too bad here, I'll sell the farm and move to sunny California and live on the beach.'

"Until that time, I had never traveled more than the distance between Logo and Pocatello. I traded my overalls and straw hat for an army uniform and helmet. I knew that the war years would be difficult, and I pleaded with Dad to use some of our savings to get a hired hand to help. He told me he would consider it, but I knew he wouldn't.

"Father borrowed Mr. Pace's wagon, and he and I traveled to Ogden, Utah, to catch the train to Fort Ord, California. I told him that I would write him from boot camp. Little did I know that it would be the last time I would ever see him.

"I wrote faithfully like I promised. After basic training, I was supposed to get a furlough before I got assigned to a permanent duty station. That didn't happen. The army needed replacements, and I received orders that I was to leave to go overseas immediately. The need for replacements was just too great. I had written to Dad letting him know that my furlough had been cancelled, and so I wouldn't be coming home soon.

"I was stationed in North Africa when at mail call I received a letter from Mr. Pace. I hadn't received a letter from my father in over four months, and I couldn't figure out how Mr. Pace's letter had gotten through, but none of my father's letters had. I opened the letter, and to my utter horror, it informed me that my father was dead. Just two weeks after that, I found myself once again on a troop ship, but this time we were heading for combat.

"I don't particularly want to talk about my combat experiences. Just take my word for it that it was horrible, and I hope that neither of my sons ever experiences the horror of war. As your mother has already told you, I got wounded, and I had to be shipped to England to be cared for. What she didn't know until I told her later, was that England was my second visit to an army hospital. I had been wounded once before."

"After we left North Africa, our company was sent directly into combat in Italy. We landed near Naples, and although the fighting was fierce, I made it through that battle without serious injury. A few days later, our platoon was assembled next to an artillery position located about a mile from the front lines, waiting for orders to advance. The huge guns were at our side. Anyway, at about noon while we were eating our rations, a resounding pop came from above me. The noise wasn't excessively loud, but I jumped, and at the same time I felt a searing pain in my back. My first thought was that I had received a powder burn and attempted to rub the place that hurt. I had no idea until later that I had been wounded. Apparently, a bullet ricocheted and struck me in the back on a downward angle. I tried to feel the spot where my back was burning, but the pain was in one of those places I simply couldn't reach.

"Just then the order was given for us to move out. We advanced as rapidly as possible toward the German bunker emplacements. There was a lot of action around us, but we were finally able to overrun the enemy position and take some prisoners. It wasn't until later that a medic, who was making his rounds, spotted a bloodstain on the back of my shirt. He lifted my shirt and told me that I had been wounded. He described my injury as being a puncture followed by a six-inch red line that extended under the skin along my shoulder blade. He could see a purple fragment under my skin. He put me face down on a gurney, and I was taken to the field hospital.

"I had raced a mile not even knowing I was wounded, and now I had no choice but to be carried away on a litter. At this point, my wound was more of an irritant than anything else. Because I had continued to fight even though I was wounded, I was given a commendation for gallantry in action. I tried to explain to my commanding officer that I didn't even know that I had been shot, but that made no difference to him.

"'You were conspicuous, and right now we need heroes,' he told me.

"A field doctor examined, poked, and prodded around the wound. The examination caused me more pain than the injury. The medic explained that the surgery to remove the bullet fragment would be similar to removing a large sliver. It only took a few seconds, and the fragment was out. The bullet had passed under my skin but had not entered my back muscles.

"More painful to me than the wound was when a medic shot me full of fluids before pouring powdered sulfur into my wound to fight infection. A couple of stitches later, I was declared ready for duty. I was transferred to a convalescent ward aboard a troop ship and stayed there for three days. It wasn't much of a wound, but the army did award me the Purple Heart. It was sitting on my pillow when I came back from using the latrine. I was assigned to a holding area for two more weeks before again being sent to the front lines.

"I was in and out of combat for the next two years. In June of 1944, I was in one of the companies that stormed the Normandy beaches in France. I was also one of the lucky ones who survived. I got through all of the really bad stuff but then got blasted four weeks later when an artillery shell landed directly behind the four-man squad I was leading. I was in front and the only one who survived.

"I was knocked unconscious, and the next five days were just a blur. When I did come to, it was all at once. I was suddenly wide-awake, not groggy in the slightest. I opened my eyes, and there was the most beautiful woman I had ever seen. I was on my stomach, and she was directly in front of me, wiping my forehead with a cold towel. The sunlight was coming through the window, and it framed her in its light. She had blond hair, big blue eyes, beautiful white teeth, and a delightful smile. When I saw her, I was sure that I had died and gone to heaven. I remembered asking her where I was, and she told me that I was in a London army hospital ward.

"I found out later that that sweet nurse had positioned my bed in such a way that when I opened my eyes, I could look out the window. I also learned that all of my injuries were in my back, buttocks, and legs and that explained why I was on always on my stomach. For my entire stay in the hospital, I ate, slept, and visited in the bottoms-up position.

"I wasn't in much pain, but what pain I did experience was in my backside. I wasn't paralyzed because I could move my toes. I never considered my wounds to be life-threatening. I could feed myself, and all food went through my system like it was supposed to. I figured I would be up and around in no time.

"Bathroom chores presented a problem for a while, but we worked out the details. If your mother wants to tell you about that, she can do it when I am not in the room."

Ruth laughed loudly and rolled her eyes.

"A week passed, and then one evening an army doctor stood next to my bed and held a photograph and an x-ray in front of me. He explained that shrapnel had hit me in twenty-seven different places. I had puncture wounds that extended from below my neck all the way to my knees. I was lucky to be alive. There were two large shrapnel punctures in my buttocks, which probably explained why they always had me lie on my stomach. The doctor showed me in the x-ray a couple of spots between my shoulder blades. He explained that he had extracted several metal particles, but two jagged pieces of shrapnel couldn't be removed because they were dangerously close to my spine.

"The doctor explained, 'The body has a remarkable capacity to correct most of its ills, and I hope that will happen in your case. Someday, when technology and equipment have improved, that metal will have to be removed, but in the meantime, we can only hope that your body will build up some protective tissue around the objects. I don't want to frighten you, but if you do experience any abnormal pain or loss of feeling, then you notify me immediately because surgery will then be necessary regardless of the outcome.'

"He told me not to do anything stupid that could make the problem worse. He assured me that if I agitated it, it could cut into my spinal cord and cause permanent paralysis or even death. The doctor continued, 'I will be keeping close tabs on your condition. A surgeon from Switzerland will arrive here soon to do some extensive surgery on other combat victims. While he is here, he is going to examine you. I have already written him about you and have sent him your medical records and x-rays.'

"Up until that very moment, I hadn't experienced any pain in my back in the spot he had just pointed out on the x-ray. But from that time on, that particular spot on my back hurt continually. Talk about the power of suggestion!

"Three more weeks passed, and then one day two men stood next to my bed. My doctor introduced the Swiss doctor to me, but the man had a name I could never pronounce. The Swiss surgeon explained that he had scheduled me for an operation the next morning. I was told to not eat or drink anything after five o'clock, and then they both just left. So much for the extensive examination and consolation I was supposed to have.

"Early the next morning, a whole company of people in white uniforms marched in and stood over me. I was pushed, prodded, and stuck with needles. The medical staff scratched their heads, massaged their goatees, and scribbled notes on clipboards. I wasn't asked one question, and as quickly as they entered, they left. Fifteen minutes after that, I was shuttled into an operating room. The last thing I remembered was someone placing a miniature gauze-covered horse collar over my nose and mouth.

"When I woke up, I was again on my stomach, but I was retching into a bowl being held by my beautiful nurse. Every pore in my body smelled like ether, and I was embarrassed to have her see me in such a pitiful condition.

"It was another two weeks before my rehabilitation started. After the surgery, I could still wiggle my toes and fingers, and that was a good sign. I spent a total of two months in that London hospital, and each day my amazing nurse helped me out of bed, and then we would walk together, first around the wings and eventually outside on the grounds.

"Time passed, we talked, and I found myself waiting in anticipation for her to appear. My nurse would grasp my elbow and steady me as we walked. Her words were always words of encouragement, and I loved her English accent."

Carl and Mike both smiled at their mother and nodded in agreement.

"Occasionally we could hear the sound of explosions and see a few German airplanes, but I knew we were far from the actual battles.

"We found ourselves sharing our experiences with each other. We were both born on October, 5 1922. We loved music, but hated opera and ballet. We liked sports—she soccer, me baseball. We liked similar books, but the biggest thing we found in common was that we were falling in love.

"Ruth was heartbroken when I received orders transferring me to an army hospital in California where my scars would be 'minimized,' I think the word was.

"Before I left England, I met with military officials and spent many hours completing all of the necessary paperwork so that after the war, I could marry Ruth in the United States. I purchased an engagement and wedding ring set, and on one of our long walks, I knelt on one knee and slipped the ring on her finger and proposed marriage. Thankfully, she accepted."

The boys looked at their mother, and she winked and smiled at them.

"Ruth stood portside as I went up the gangplank to the troop carrier that would take me to California. We both knew that it might be a long time before I would see her again, but we promised to write, and we both knew in our hearts that someday our marriage would take place. I needed to find a job, earn enough money to bring your mother to America, and find a place for us to live. I figured that it would take about five years.

"Your mother never questioned coming to the States. Her family was gone, she had no one left in England, and London was in rubble. She wanted to start a new life, and so long as it was with me, she seemed to be content.

"It took four weeks of zigzagging by troop ship to get from England to California. After getting to San Francisco, I took a two-hour train ride to get to an army hospital in Modesto. After reporting in, I was assigned quarters, took a long shower, and was then given two months' back pay. My doctor gave me a letter allowing me a furlough. I was instructed to remain in full dress uniform and to be back no later than midnight ten days later. I stowed my excess gear in my room and was on a bus two hours later bound for Ogden, Utah.

"I hadn't been to Pocatello since the day I rode in the wagon with my dad to bury Mom and Michael. I felt both an obligation and a desire to visit their grave sites and pay my respects to them and to my grandparents. And I also wanted to visit with Uncle James and Aunt Lydia, who both had been so good to my dad and me.

"I had been given instructions on how to care for my injuries in case I had a problem. I promised my doctor that I would for sure be back within ten days.

"When I got to Ogden, I used a portion of my back pay to purchase a beat-up 1937 Ford truck. It cost me sixty-five dollars, and I sure hoped it would make it all the way to Preston! I threw my duffel bag into the bed of the pickup and headed for southern Idaho.

"The war with Japan was still going on, but Germany had surrendered, and we all hoped that it wouldn't be long before the fighting in the Pacific would come to an end. I wouldn't be discharged until after the war ended, so I hoped it would be soon. I had already been told that my injuries would prevent me from seeing more combat.

"The dented and rusted truck worked fine, and the trip only took two hours before I passed through the main street of Preston City. Thirty minutes later, our old farm was in sight. It was now mine, but I certainly didn't want to start farming again. My health just wasn't up to the rigors of working the land.

"The old shacks were still in the same place. They were a memory of a time long ago. This crude shelter had been a happy home for me, but without my dad, I had no desire to live there.

"As I looked across the road at the farm, the ground looked more fertile and productive than I had remembered it. In the distance was a man seated on a tractor, and I was surprised that someone would be farming my land. I decided to sort that all out later.

"I drove across the gravel roadway that divided our farm from that of the neighbors. Parking the truck, I walked across the field. I spotted the old maple tree where Dad and I used to rest and visit while we ate our lunch. I headed there and sat down in its shade. The man on the tractor shut off his engine and walked toward me. I didn't recognize him, but I stood up and waited for him.

"The stranger spoke, and I remember the conversation well. 'When I saw the truck stop and a man in uniform get out, I thought it might be you. You are Bill Spader, aren't you?' the man asked.

"Extending my hand, I told him that I was. He introduced himself as David Jefferson Lee and explained that my father and he had been good friends.

"David continued, 'After Samuel's death, I took over the farm and worked it along with my own. I simply couldn't stand seeing such a good piece of land go idle, so I set up a bank account under the name of William Spader and me in Preston. I have been fair and honest, and all I could hope for is that someday you would return safely, and today you did. I have kept an accurate record of income and expenses. I hope that you will be pleased with the results.'

"Naturally, I was surprised to learn that I had been David's partner for the past four years. David went on. 'I relocated to Idaho four years ago shortly after my wife's death. I had some money, so I purchased most of the adjoining land. Being new to the area, I came over to introduce myself to Samuel. He was fiddling around with that old tractor. The tractor was small, ancient, and looked like it might fall apart at any minute. Anyway, my tractor was new, and it could run circles around his. I could see he needed help, so I offered to plow his field, but Samuel bristled at the very suggestion. He was way too proud to let someone else take care of his duties.'

"'I was smart enough to recognize my blunder, and I quickly came up with a solution. I told him that I needed someone to supervise the transient workers come harvest time. If Samuel would be willing to boss the workers during that time, then in exchange I would plow his field. That was a proposal that Samuel could accept, and he did.

"'We hit if off then, and from that day until the day he died, we were good friends. We were about the same age, were both farmers, and we each had a son serving in the military. Your pop didn't own an automobile, so I made it a point of driving over to his place. He was good company, and most every evening we played checkers, popped some corn, read the Bible, told a few tall tales, but mostly we proudly talked about our sons,' David told me.

"David's wife had passed away five years earlier, and his two daughters were grown and had families of their own. He had hoped that at least one of them would have lived closer by, but that wasn't to be. He told me that one of the saddest days of his life came when he learned from the War Department that his son had been killed in combat. Kenneth was a marine and had died early in 1942 on some unnamed island in the Pacific. What was left of his body was shipped to Hawaii and buried in a veteran's cemetery.

"David also told me that when his son died, Samuel was the one person who truly seemed to understand his loss and greatly comforted him in his most difficult times. Through those tribulations, they became the best of friends.

"'As I look back now, Samuel was probably the most caring and only real friend I ever had. I loved him like a brother,' David said.

"David told me that when Samuel got a letter from me, he would read it aloud to him. It was Dad's way of letting him share in my life, and somehow that seemed to soften David's loss. Dad only received three of my letters while I was overseas, and David told me that he cherished each of them. David said that one afternoon he had intercepted the postman so that he could deliver my letter to Dad himself.

"David told me, 'I spotted your dad on his knees, once again working on that darn tractor. As usual, it wasn't running well, and Samuel was trying to crank it up. When I got closer, I held up the letter and shouted a greeting to Samuel. He looked up, smiled, and waved. When I was no more than ten feet from him, he got to his feet and then got a strange, puzzled look on his face. He squinted, wrinkled his forehead, and then toppled facedown in the dirt. I ran to his side, but he wasn't breathing. I carried him to my truck and raced to Preston, but he never regained consciousness. The doctor said that Samuel apparently had a brain clot and died instantly.'

"David told me that none of my letters included a return address, so he hadn't been able to write and tell me about my father's death. He had opened and read my letters, hoping to get a hint of how to reach me. None of us were allowed to put on a return address or give our location in any of our mail home.

"David went on, 'Your dad had once spoken to me about wanting to be buried in Pocatello next to his wife, son, and parents, so when he died, I made the arrangements to get his body to Pocatello.

"'I found the cemetery and placed Samuel next to Gretchen and Michael. Your grandparents, Ezra and Nancy, were also buried nearby, as was Samuel's brother James and his wife Lydia. I made the necessary arrangements, purchased a casket, and bought a headstone for your dad plus a larger family headstone for the Spader clan. I hired a couple of men to dig a grave and then knelt and offered a prayer at the grave site before the grave was filled in,' David said.

"It wasn't until that moment that I learned that my aunt and uncle were dead, and I felt a real regret that I hadn't been able to visit with them. They had been so good to my father, my grandparents, and me."

Speaking directly to his children, Bill said, "When my time comes, it is my desire to be buried in that same Pocatello cemetery. I own a full lot that will accommodate eight of us, if it happens to be the desire of the rest of my family.

"I offered to pay David, but he waved off my offer. He was honored to have the privilege of paying respect to his dearest friend. He had boxed up everything worth saving from Dad's house and put it in his granary under some protective canvas. The bed and dresser and other stuff in the shack weren't worth much, so he had either sold it or given it to needy people. He told me that all of my letters, as well as the undelivered ones my father had sent to me, were in one of the storage boxes. He explained that most of the equipment had been too rusty to use, and he sold the lot to a junkyard for two hundred dollars. He felt that he got the best of the deal even at that.

"I later spent several hours reading the letters and recalling all of the glorious times I had spent with my father. I still have those letters, and they mean very much to me.

"David then told me a little more about the farm. He had learned that the government was going to need beans for the servicemen, and so he put his farm and mine into beans. His gamble was a good one because the government paid him a pretty fair price for the crops. He told me that he had deducted my share of the cost of seed from my share of the income, but everything else was in my bank account in Preston—an account up until a few moments earlier, I never knew even existed.

"He asked me if I intended to start farming again, but I told him that I did not. I explained that the only reason I stayed on the farm was to help my father. Now that he was gone, I had other plans. I told David that I had fallen in love with an English nurse. It was my plan to get myself all healed, find a good-paying job, and then send for my lovely wife-to-be and get married. Knowing that, he gave me some options about what he thought I could do with the farm. He said that I could sell the farm to him or to someone else, or I could continue to be his partner.

"I again thanked him for taking care of the farm and asked him to name his own price for the land. He told me that irrigated land was selling between thirty and eighty dollars an acre. He offered to give me eighty dollars. I countered with fifty, and we settled for sixty-five. We shook hands, and the deal was done. Mr. David Lee was a remarkable gentleman, and I told him so.

"I told David that I had wanted to visit with Mr. and Mrs. Pace and would accompany him to Preston to sign over the farm. We set up a meeting time and shook hands again. I wanted to get everything done soon so I could get to Pocatello before dark.

"Mr. and Mrs. Pace were on the front porch of their home when I rolled down the gravel driveway. I stopped, but neither of them appeared to be alarmed or surprised. It was just an everyday experience for these wonderful people to have unannounced visitors. I got out of the truck and walked toward their porch, and when recognition hit them, they jumped to their feet and wrapped me in their arms.

"I told them that I had wanted to visit with them before going to the Pocatello cemetery to pay my respects to those there. I gave them an overview of my travels in foreign lands and let them know a little about the injuries I had received but assured them that I was now doing fine. I excitedly let them know about my beautiful Ruth and our plans for the future. I also summarized the contents of my conversation with David. They were very complimentary of him.

"We talked for another fifteen minutes before I explained that it was time for me to leave so I could get the land signed over to

David before heading out. Al Pace walked with me to the truck. As I got ready to leave, Al grasped my shoulders to give me a hug when he noticed the ribbons on my army jacket. He stood back, and his eyes filled with tears. He had served in France during World War I and was familiar with the various commendations given to servicemen.

"'I didn't know you had seen so much combat,' he told me.

"I nodded and said no more. He hugged me, walked slowly back to his wife and slumped wearily into his rocker next to her. He didn't try to explain the reason for his feelings—he would probably do that after I left.

"David was waiting at the side of the road when I came back to the farm. Since we would be going in different directions after our meeting with the bank, he suggested that we drive separately. Twenty minutes later, we were seated in an office in the courthouse, and ten minutes after that, I was no longer a landowner. But I was considerably wealthier than I had been when I entered the building. I was handed a cashier's check made out to me in the amount of $5,200. It was the most money I had ever handled, and it now meant that I could afford to get married and bring my beloved Ruth to the United States. I was in heaven at that moment.

"The two of us then walked over to the Preston Bank, and David introduced me to the president. David explained that I already had an account there but that I would be closing it out. I had no idea what to expect when my account book was opened before me, but for the second time in less than an hour, I was once again overwhelmed.

"The account balance was over $8,750. Added to the money I had received from the sale of the land, I had nearly $14,000 in my trembling hands. My voice quivered as I thanked the bank official. Once outside, I grasped David in my arms and openly wept. I told him that I now had enough money to bring my bride-to-be to the States. We wouldn't have to wait five years. With luck, we could be married within two months.

"David and I shook hands, and then I got back in my truck. My knees were shaking, and I had trouble shifting the gears. David stood on the sidewalk and waved and laughed.

"Arriving in Pocatello three hours later, I easily found the cemetery. After purchasing several bouquets of flowers, I headed for my parents' graves. The place was easy to find because of the seven-foot-high Spader family marker that David had provided. The marker stood majestically in view.

"I sat near the graves of my parents and brother and spoke to them as if we were having an evening chat in the parlor. My words flowed as I told them of my love for them, about the war and my bride-to-be, and of the kindness of David Lee. After putting flowers on all five graves, I started my journey back to the hospital in California.

"I had only been back in the hospital for eight weeks when the war finally ended. There was a huge celebration throughout California and the rest of the world. It was especially significant to those of us who were still in the service and under medical care. Our discharge wouldn't come until after the doctors said we were fit to enter civilian life again.

"Each day, I was bathed, scraped, sanded, and treated, and then one day the chief of staff at the hospital entered my quarters and pulled up a chair. 'Captain Spader!' he uttered. 'We here at the hospital are all satisfied with the surgical repair work we have done on you back and legs. Our work has progressed as far as medical science currently allows. I am going to issue you a hospital release, but it will be necessary for you to come back here or to another army hospital every two months for a routine examination. I hereby extend to you our congratulations along with an honorable discharge from this United States Army.'

"I was handed an envelope that contained $400 severance pay and a note attached to the medical document identifying names and addresses of all VA hospitals in the United States. I bid farewell to the doctors, nurses, and my fellow soldiers and then hopped into my trusty Ford and left Modesto. Except for a couple of short stops, I drove straight through to Boise, Idaho. I tossed around the idea of purchasing a new vehicle, but the old Ford had been so reliable, I simply could not part with it. Besides, I wasn't about to spend any of my new fortune on anything until Ruth was by my side. Since I had already completed the citizenship paperwork, the visa and travel permit for Ruth was in process. It would take five years before she could become a citizen, but we could both wait.

"Then a strange and wonderful thing happened. Somehow the governor of the state of Idaho got wind of my situation, and through cooperation with the United States Secretary of State and the War Department, I was informed that if my bride and I could be married immediately. They would allow us to be married in the United States, and Ruth would be given a visa that was good for five years."

The Bride

"Two months later, on February 12, 1946, I met my beautiful bride-to-be at the docks in New York City. Standing next to her was the governor of the state of Idaho and an Idaho State congressman. On Valentine's Day, two days later, we were married in a quiet ceremony by a New York justice of the peace. My newly acquired wealth allowed us to spend two full weeks exploring New York State. We visited the big city, then journeyed to Niagara Falls, and even made a short visit in Montreal and Quebec City before catching a train that took us to Boston and then to Pocatello.

"By the way, your mother had to wait for five years before she was granted full US citizenship, but when she did, that was also a wonderful day. She knows more about the United States Constitution and Bill of Rights than most lawyers.

"After our honeymoon, I planned to find a good-paying job, but that was easier said than done. There were many other veterans in Idaho who were also looking for work. When the war finally ended, most of the soldiers, sailors, and marines returned home en masse. For those of us who came home, it was magnificent. Unfortunately, there were many others who didn't come home at all.

"Women had to take over in the workforce while we were gone, but now that we were back, many of these women didn't want to give up their jobs. They had gotten used to being self-sufficient. And I didn't blame them. They kept our economy going while we were gone, but it didn't help our situation to not be able to find work.

"Many of the employers who had cheered us when we went off to war were now reluctant to hire us back. Production advancements had progressed so rapidly that many veterans were now simply not qualified enough to get their old jobs back, and many of their old jobs no longer existed. Your mother and I felt that we could bide our time until I could find a good-paying job. We had all of the dollars from the farm plus several hundred dollars more that I got in military severance pay. Our bank account was nearly $13,000. In those days, that much money would buy and furnish a house, farm, livestock, and two hundred acres of prime irrigated land. Because I hadn't found work, your mother and I decided to hold on to our savings and live frugally. My back and upper legs were still giving me some problems, and although I did qualify for disability pay from the government, it was only a token amount of sixty-two dollars and fifty cents a month. I had initially been under the impression that the amount would be much larger. It certainly helped out, but it wasn't enough to sustain us, so it was important that I find work.

"While at an employment office, a fellow veteran told me about a program that would allow me to enter college even though I had never finished high school. I decided to check it out. As it turned out, I was able to obtain a part-time custodial position in a Pocatello bank. The income from that janitorial job added to my disability pay let us have enough money to rent a small apartment and put food on the table. I enrolled in a special veterans education program in Pocatello, and with the help of your mother and several government-provided tutors, I was able to take high school and college classes concurrently. The state of Idaho made many concessions, and I received my high school diploma."

Carl looked at Mike in amazement and whispered a little too loudly, "I didn't think that Dad even finished high school, let alone attend college."

Ruth was still fuming at his outburst earlier in the evening, but she did manage a curt nod to her eldest son.

"Your mother is really a smart lady, and she could type up a storm. She helped me with much of my college homework. I would tell her what I wanted to say, and she would put it down on paper. I also found that my military service seemed to carry weight with most of my teachers and professors. The physical education classes, mandatory for most students, were waived for all veterans. I guess the university administrators figured that if we could crawl around Europe and Asia for two or three years dodging bullets, we could probably pass a tennis or bowling class. I did work hard to complete all my assignments, but I know that many special allowances were made on my behalf.

"Later I gave up my custodial job when I found a full-time job closer to our home. I was working nights hefting sacks of potatoes into trucks, and for two more years I went to school during the daylight hours and worked nights at the dock. I only got about six hours of sleep a night, but everything was working out, and we were actually adding money to our savings.

"Then it happened. In mid-June 1948, I was lifting a potato sack onto the bed of a truck when I felt a sudden catch in my back. The pain was excruciating. My knees buckled, and I fell to the ground. I was rushed by ambulance to the nearest hospital. My back was x-rayed, and an alert technician discovered a small piece of metal imbedded next to my spine. He later told me that the object was about the size of a kernel of corn.

"The army was notified because I was a veteran, and for reasons unknown to me, the decision was made to transport me to a naval hospital in San Diego. A partially paralyzed soldier in a hospital filled with sailors and marines—how was I to survive?

"Apparently, the large fragments of metal that the Swiss doctor removed from my back had overshadowed the smaller piece that was still in me. Had I been in any pain or shown any signs of a problem, the army doctors in England would have most certainly checked it out, but they thought I was fine, and so did I. As a result, I was shipped back to the United States. I had been in several hospitals, primarily to have skin grafts and other cosmetic surgeries to cover my scarred back and legs. No one ever considered that I might have bigger problem.

"When I was shipped off to San Diego, I couldn't walk. Ruth moved to California to be near me. My veteran benefits gave my wife commissary privileges, so her food was rather inexpensive, but lodging near the hospital was terribly expensive. We knew we could make it because we still had all of our savings. With over $13,000 in the bank and no debts, we knew that at any time, we could pay cash for nice house, car, and have gobs of money left for the frivolous things in life like vacations and a boat.

"The navy did help your mother find a small couple's apartment located near the hospital, and she moved right in. Being back in a hospital was very upsetting to me. I had no feeling below my rib cage. I could still breathe and use my hands, but the rest of my body was useless. I was devastated and wondered how such a small sliver of metal could cause me that much of a problem? All of my medical costs were covered because my injury was sustained in combat, but that wasn't helping pay for the bills that were mounting up at home. To make things even worse, your mother couldn't work because she was four months pregnant and very ill.

"I had a total of seven surgeries while in the hospital, and I was in a body cast and flat on my stomach for fourteen months. I wasn't improving, and my legs and hips were atrophying. All I wanted to do was die, and there were times that I actually prayed that I would. I knew my life was over and I had no future. I wouldn't be able to play with my child. We wouldn't have more children, and my mental attitude was really low. During one of her visits, I suggested to your mother that she should divorce me and create a life for herself. That was the only time I have been really close to an enraged Englishwoman. It was something frightening to behold, and it is a thing that I hope neither of you boys ever experiences.

"One morning I woke up with the sensation that my left foot was cold. I strained my neck to look to see that my left foot was uncovered and in a draft. I had feeling! I tried to wiggle my toes, and my big toe visibly moved. I screamed for a nurse, and a flock of them came running into my room. They must have thought that I was dying. I showed them that I could wiggle my toe, and they exploded with laughter and delight. The doctors were summoned. After countless weeks of therapy and rehabilitation, I was finally able, with assistance, to stand on a scale. I weighed a scant 120 pounds.

"Anyway, from that time on, I started to get more movement and feeling. I started to enjoy food, and I could see the potential for a life. In total, I was in that hospital for twenty-seven months. Each day, I would do my exercises and get my physical therapy. I was getting stronger, but still far from strong. By the time I was released, I was within fifteen pounds of what I weighed when I checked into the hospital, but I was one inch shorter. The day I collapsed on the dock, I stood six feet two inches tall and weighed 216 pounds, all muscle.

"It was necessary for Ruth and me to live in San Diego because the doctors wanted me to be near the hospital. Much rehabilitation and repair work still had to be done. We were thankful that we hadn't purchased all of the things we initially had on our want list. As I said, my medical bills were all paid for by the government, but during this time, your mother's expenses had to come out of our savings account.

"I had never wanted your mother to work and had literally insisted that she stay home. I was selfish because I wanted my partner and companion waiting at home for me when I got off work. I wanted to eat home-cooked meals, sleep in clean sheets, and wear pressed shirts. I wanted to be near her all of the time. I loved her. Even though she was pregnant and ill a lot of the time, she got a part-time job at the naval hospital child-care unit. The center was close enough she could catch a bus that stopped in front of the hospital. Your mother was a registered nurse, and her qualifications were sorely needed. She worked there four months until November 2, 1947 the day you were born, Carl. She came to work that day, but she didn't even have time to punch the time clock before her water broke. She was placed in a wheelchair and rushed to the delivery room. You were actually born in the naval hospital. You, your mother, and I were all residents of the same hospital for a few days.

"Carl, when you came into the world, you were having trouble breathing. We had no medical insurance, and my GI insurance only provided money to my family in case of death. Since I had been officially discharged from the army, there was no allowance for families. Although you were ill, Carl, you couldn't stay in the naval hospital because I was no longer on active duty. Three days after you were born, you were transferred by ambulance to a private hospital located about ten miles from our home. You stayed there for seven more weeks before they would let your mother take you home. Every day your mother would catch a bus and visit you, and then visit me at our respective hospitals. I couldn't even be with your mother when you were born. Hospital regulations wouldn't allow Ruth to bring you in to see me, so you were seventeen months old before I ever saw anything but a photo of you!

"When I was finally released, your mother brought our baby with her to the hospital in a taxi, and I sat in the backseat of that same taxi and held you all the way to our apartment. The taxi driver was very emotional and wouldn't take a cent in fare.

"Your first few years were really touch and go. You required constant care, and that made it impossible to hire a babysitter. Your mother had to always be with you, so she had to give up her nursing job at the hospital. For the first six months of your life, if you turned over onto your back, you would quit breathing. You had to sleep on your stomach, and every two hours your mother would have to pound on your back to dislodge mucus. When she came to the hospital to visit me, she brought you along all bundled up regardless of the weather outside. You were so precious, and we didn't want to lose you. It was against hospital regulations to allow any child under twelve into a patient's room, so she would take you to the newborn center, and one sweet nurse would care for you for a half hour while your mother visited me.

"I had been given doctor's orders that I was not to do anything strenuous for six months. After that time I was to get a complete examination and evaluation. Fortunately, your mother got pregnant again. I won't go into how that happened, but maybe some day when you boys are older and have children of your own, I will share the details.

"My education was directed toward being a teacher, but at that time, I wouldn't have been a prime candidate for employment. I could have been a typist, but I couldn't type. I maybe could have been a lawyer, but I liked people, so I couldn't do that either."

Ruth and the boys all laughed.

"The apartment that you and your mother had been staying in was a 'couples only' unit, but the landlord and neighbors had made an exception because I was in the hospital. When I got out, that exception was negated, and we were kindly but quickly evicted.

"We found the place we are living in now. It wasn't something we wanted, but it was the only thing we could afford that had more than one bedroom. We moved in what furniture we had, and if you look around you, most of it is still here. Those patio chairs in our backyard were some I bought from a vendor one day when your mother and I were at the beach. They cost us one dollar each.

"Your mother found work at the nursing home where she is still employed. The nearby location made it possible for her to work full-time because there was a good woman living next door to the nursing home who would inexpensively tend children. When you boys got older and entered school, your mother reduced her work schedule to twenty-four hours a week so she could be with you when you went to school and got home. Without that extra cash, we would be even worse off than we are. I think the only reason they gave her that many hours is that they like to hear her English accent."

The boys once again laughed.

"There was an old man who used to live next door who worked as a custodian at an apartment complex. He was going to retire, and he put in a good word for me. I jumped at the chance and got the job before it was even advertised. It doesn't pay much either, but your mother and I pool our paychecks, and we survive. Each day we pray for better times.

"I don't think my back will ever be totally right, but we hope it will. I am sorry, oh so sorry, that we can't afford to get you some of the things that we know you want and need, but now you know why. Did I leave anything out, sweetheart?"

"You sure did," Ruth replied. "Your father sort of skipped over a few details. He never told you much about his military experiences, only that he served. What you don't know is that he is a highly decorated veteran. He won't talk about it, so I will. Your father was in the army and was wounded—that you know. What you don't know was that he received a battlefield commission while he was fighting in Europe. He was promoted from sergeant to captain, and that doesn't happen often. Remember, at that time, he only had a tenth grade education.

"You have always thought your father was uneducated. I don't know where you picked up that idea, but I hope the misconception has been squelched after hearing what you have been told. Your father told you that he was to get his diploma but didn't because of the injury. He always wanted to teach school, but he knew that his lack of education would be a limiting factor. Before we were married, I used to walk the hospital grounds with him in England. He would continually talk about teaching kids. He loved to see kids learn.

"Because of his valor, the governor of the state of Idaho granted him an honorary high school diploma. He had completed about half of the graduation requirements through military extension courses, but it was still a great honor they bestowed upon him. With it came a waiver to attend Idaho State University or the University of Idaho if he so desired, and he so desired. Idaho State University accepted him with open arms, and he was given forty hours credit waiver toward his degree as a reward for his service of his country. He was given money from the government for tuition and books under the GI bill. Then of all things, several wealthy potato farmers learned about your father's desire to go to college, and as a group they donated a sizable amount of cash and awarded him a full scholarship to cover his housing and family expenses while he attended school. That's what people in Idaho thought of your father.

"Don't ever blame your father for our financial situation because what has drained our savings and prevented us from getting ahead is your father's refusal to accept welfare or compromise his integrity.

"After he graduated from Idaho State University, the state offered your father a one-year contract to teach geography in summer school at the university. It wasn't going to pay much, but it was a way for him to get his foot into the educational door. Your father accepted that offer but never got the chance to teach. He was to begin teaching classes on July 3, 1948. His reoccurring war injury prevented that from ever happening.

"Carl, one of the reasons we are broke is because your father always paid his bills, regardless of what sacrifice that meant. When you were in that hospital those seven weeks after you were born, your father used the last of our savings to pay the hospital over $4,000. He just wrote out a check that was practically all of the money we had at the time. We came to San Diego with money in our pockets. I couldn't work full-time because my priceless new baby needed special care and had special needs. It cost about three hundred dollars a month for rent, utilities, clothing, food, diapers, and other living expenses. The private hospital charges were more than $1,500 a month. When your father was finally discharged from the hospital, we had $400 to our name."

Bill tried to stop her, but she wouldn't be stopped.

"We want you to know that you were worth it, and we would be willing to do anything for you. It might also help you realize why we don't drive a new car, one that has windows that roll all the way down in the backseat and one where the springs don't protrude through the horse blanket," Ruth said.

"One more thing, and then you can all go to bed. Your father has a million-dollar mind, but it is housed in a ten-dollar body. His strength and stamina were lost because he made the conscious decision to serve his country. You can exercise, work, run, or whatever, but when parts of your body are shot away, you don't get stronger or more resilient. You just don't!"

Bill didn't want the evening to end on a sour note, so he stood and held out his arms for his sons to come to him. They hugged, but Carl was in tears and couldn't speak.

Just before Carl left to go to bed with a smile on his face, he asked one more question. "What ever happened to the Ford truck you drove to Boise?"

Bill laughed. "I drove the truck to the airport and sold it to the parking attendant for twenty dollars. The young fellow paid me in cash for it, and I printed out a bill of sale on the back of a Cracker Jack box that was in the backseat. It was the only piece of paper either of us could find."

Carl had trouble sleeping that night, and he kept thinking about his father's comment about Mr. Pace crying when he saw the ribbons. *Why should that make a grown man cry?* Carl wondered.

Carl heard water running in the kitchen, so he got out of bed to see if his mother might still be up. She was, and he sat down at the kitchen table. She could see that he was concerned and sat beside him.

"Mother, why did Mr. Pace cry when he saw the ribbons on Father's uniform?"

Ruth pondered the question for a moment before answering. "Today, while I am at work, I think it might be good if you and Mike go to the library and use that free card of yours once. I want you to see the librarian and ask her where to find books about World War II. Scan the indexes, and look for references to William Samuel Spader. We will talk about what you find this evening. It's getting late, son, so you get yourself back into bed, and don't wake your father. He really needs to have his rest," she admonished.

Just before Carl left, Ruth came to him and gave him a motherly hug.

Revelation

Early the next morning while the boys were getting dressed, Carl told Mike about the conversation he had with their mother the previous evening.

"Mom suggested that I go to the library today, and I wondered if you wanted to go with me," Carl asked.

Mike nodded his acceptance to the invitation.

"The bike still has a flat tire. Are you planning to walk?" Mike asked.

"Nope!" Carl replied. "Mom left a quarter sitting on my shirt, and since it will only cost us a nickel each way to the library, there is enough for bus fare for both of us."

Both boys were excited about going to the library. I will actually use my never-before-used library card," Carl sheepishly proclaimed.

Mike snickered.

Morning greetings were exchanged. The family ate breakfast together, and there was no mention of the tensions that had briefly existed the evening before. It was only six o'clock, so their mother wouldn't leave for work for another half hour. She would work for seven hours and be home by two.

"What have you two men got planned for today?" Bill cheerfully asked.

"Mike and I thought we would check out the library," Carl said as he held up his shiny library card. "Then Mike, and I will probably play some volleyball at the beach."

"You two are both going to the library?" Bill questioned while exhibiting an exaggerated look of amazement. "I think I had better notify our doctor. He should definitely know about this."

Conversation was light, and it wasn't long before Carl's mother was combing into place her last few strands of stubborn hair.

"You gentlemen have a productive day, and I will see you later this afternoon. Love you all!"

Bill reminded the boys that he would take a nap around noon so he would be rested for his work at three.

"Have a great day and I am looking forward to spending some time with both of you now that school is out," Bill said.

Carl and Mike downed the last of their toast and raced each other to the bathroom. Their father was sitting in a lawn chair on the back porch sunning when the boys were ready to leave.

"See you later!" both boys shouted in unison.

They walked down the steep hill and dodged traffic to get to the bus stop on the other side of the road. One transfer got them to the center of town and close to the library. Carl was a little nervous. He had been in the library only once before on a field trip with his classmates. He didn't know what to look for then, and he sure didn't know where to start now.

"What are we looking for?" Mike asked.

"Mother said to go to the World War II history section and look up William Spader's name."

Mike had been to the library several times with his mother and once with his school class. He walked quickly toward the librarian's desk. For several minutes the boys stood near the desk, waiting for the middle-aged woman to help them. The woman wore a long black knit dress with long sleeves and white ruffles around the wrists. Her long pointed nose supported tiny spectacles. Although she occasionally glanced at the boys, she made no attempt to assist them. Carl became impatient and spoke rather loudly. "Pardon me, lady, but could you please help us?"

The woman jerked upright from her chair and headed toward Carl. "This is a library, young man, and if you speak, you do it in a quiet voice! You are not the only person in this building who needs help, and when I am through with what I am doing, I will help you. Go sit down on the bench and be quiet," she harshly whispered.

Fifteen minutes passed before the woman reluctantly motioned for them to approach her desk. "Now, what do you need?" she impatiently questioned.

"We are looking for books about World War II," Mike responded.

"Over there." She pointed with her long gnarled index finger. You will find hundreds of books and magazine articles about various wars. On the table are the index books. Is that plain enough for you to follow?" she asked.

Carl was visibly angry, but Mike wisely thanked the librarian and headed for the index table.

Mike found a large reference book identified as WWII. Quickly leafing through the alphabetical listing, he was surprised to find their father's name. There it was, Spader, William Morgan, and opposite his name in the margin were three reference numbers.

Neither boy had pencil or paper, so Carl retrieved a piece of scrap notepaper from a trash can and borrowed a pencil from the only person in the reading room who wasn't frowning. He thanked the young woman and promised to quickly return it.

Mike read off the reference numbers, and Carl jotted them down.

"Now we need to go to the locator file," Mike said.

Carl read the number, and Mike thumbed through the cards until he found the first reference. Mike tugged at the card, but it was held in place with a metal rod projecting the full length of the drawer.

"I hate to do it, but I think we need to get some help from the librarian to find the books," Mike reluctantly said.

Without hesitation, Carl removed the drawer from the cabinet and carried it to the librarian's desk. The librarian gave him a disgusted look and angrily snatched the drawer from Carl's hands. She walked to the locator file and shoved the drawer into the cabinet.

In a raspy, chastising whisper, she pointed to a number on the card. "This is locator identification, and if you are going to have the privilege of using this library, then you better soon learn how to read this card," she barked.

"Yes, ma'am," Carl said.

She pointed her thumb to a long row of books neatly stacked in matching bookshelves. "Those books all have something to do with wars. The sign above the books will plainly tell you which section deals with World War II. Didn't your teachers ever bring you here and show you how to use the library?"

Carl looked sheepishly at the floor while Mike distanced himself from the discussion by nonchalantly looking out a window. Neither boy answered the question.

"You have your locator numbers, now find them in the locator file and write down the corresponding title. Do not remove this drawer again," she scolded as she paced back to her desk.

"Wow," Carl whispered. "I sure don't want to marry a librarian when I grow up."

With the required information in hand, the brothers commenced their search through the myriad of books. It took them nearly ten minutes to find the first book on their list. It was in the correct section but was not filed in correct alphabetical order.

"I bet the old witch filed this book in the wrong place just because she knew we were going to be looking for it," Mike speculated.

After several minutes of searching, all three books were located. Carrying the heavy books, they tiptoed quietly to a far corner of the library. The boys wanted to get as far away from the librarian as they could.

They sat at the same side of the table, and Carl opened the first book. The index showed that William Morgan Spader's name was listed on four separate pages.

The first of the four reference pages listed the names of every member of the armed services who participated in the invasion of Normandy, France, on June 6, 1944. There were many pages of names, and their father's name was there. A small *w* or *k* designated those who had been wounded or killed. William's name reflected that he had been wounded.

The second reference page listed the names of those individuals who had been awarded medals by the French government. Only a Frenchman could pronounce the names of the medals. Again their father's name was listed.

The next reference provided the names of servicemen who had received the Bronze Star. Again their father's name was listed. A lead-in paragraph predetermined the criteria for the award.

> The Bronze Star is awarded to a person, who, while a member of the armed services distinguished himself or herself conspicuously in the face of the enemy resistance, above and beyond the call of duty while engaged in an action against an enemy of the United States.

"Wow," Carl said. "I had no idea."

The fourth page was the one that took away their breaths.

The lead paragraph indicated that during World War II, there had been 441 Congressional Medal of Honor recipients, most posthumously.

"What does *posthumously* mean?" Mike asked.

"It means they got the award after they were dead," Carl replied.

The qualification for the award was also identified.

> The Congressional Medal of Honor is awarded in the name of Congress to a person who, while a member of the armed forces, distinguished himself or herself

conspicuously by gallantry and intrepidity at the risk of life above and beyond the call of duty while engaged in an action against an enemy of the United States; while engaged in military operations involving conflicts with an opposing foreign force; or while serving with friendly foreign forces engaged in an armed conflict against an opposing armed force in which the United States is not a belligerent party. The deed performed must have been one of personal bravery or self-sacrifice so conspicuous as to clearly distinguish the individual above his or her comrades and must have involved risk of life. Incontestable proof of the performance of service is required, and each recommendation for award of this decoration is considered on the standard of extraordinary merit.

There in the middle of the page was the name of William Morgan Spader. Both boys slumped low in their chairs, eyes wide and mouths open.

"Our father was awarded the Congressional Medal of Honor, and he never even told us!" Carl exclaimed.

The brothers were overwhelmed. They were in so much awe of their father that tears started to stream from their eyes.

"Why wouldn't he have told us about that?" Mike asked.

In the next reference book they opened, they found their father's name under the section entitled "Congressional Medal of Honor Winners."

There were two full-color photos of their father. The first photo was of William in a full-dress uniform with the Medal of Honor suspended around his neck. The second photo was of him in the army hospital in England. He was sitting up in bed as a United States senator from the state of Idaho placed the medal around his neck on behalf of President Franklin Roosevelt. The subsequent page described what their father had done to receive the award.

On or about 0700, June 6, 1944, Sergeant William Morgan Spader, though pinned down by hostile enemy fire, led twelve members of his squad through a heavily mined area on Omaha Beach in order to secure a beachhead position. Sergeant Spader instructed his men to follow his footprints in the sand as he led them through the minefield. During the next two hours, he conspicuously and gallantly fought, and although seriously wounded and heavily outnumbered by the enemy, he inspired soldiers to advance. On four separate occasions, Sergeant Spader led charges against machine gun emplacements and was successful in overpowering each of the enemy positions. After breaking through the barricade, he positioned his platoon and returned to the beach to assist other soldiers by providing fire cover and helping the wounded to reach safety. At the risk of his own life and facing almost certain death, his actions resulted in not only overpowering an adversary, but in the process, he saved the lives of a countless number of his comrades in arms.

During the beach assault, all four of Sergeant Spader's superior officers were either seriously wounded or killed. During that engagement, Sergeant Spader received a battlefield commission and officially assumed the position of company commander. He continued in that capacity for nine days until he was relieved. He assumed command of his company and continued leading them for four more weeks until he himself was seriously wounded and was relocated to an army hospital for treatment.

The boys opened the third book, but it contained information almost identical to the text of the other two.

For a long time, the brothers excitedly discussed this new information about their father. He looked exceptionally handsome in his uniform, but how little they knew about this great man— and he was their father.

They were still looking at the books and talking when the librarian walked up to them. "You two are making a lot of noise, and I am afraid I will have to ask you to leave. The library is a place to come and read, not look at pictures and visit. I would suggest that you come back another day after you have had time to think about your actions," she stated.

At that moment, Carl was having trouble controlling his emotions. Rather than speak and most likely be banned forever from using the library, he simply swiveled the book toward her.

"This is our father, and we are very proud of him." With his teeth grit together, he asked, "Do you want us to put the books back in the correct place, or should we just leave them here so you can put them just anywhere you can reach?"

Neither the librarian nor the boys had anything more they wanted to say. They closed the books reverently and stacked them neatly on the table then quietly stood and headed for the exit. They held their heads high and walked with confidence and a countenance of pride as if they had just discovered that they were born of royalty.

"Wow, our father won the Medal of Honor," whispered Mike after exiting the library. They headed for the bus stop but mutually agreed that they couldn't wait for that old bus; they were too excited. The run home took them less than twenty minutes. Any idea of playing volleyball was out of our minds. They were too excited to talk coherently; they just rambled and giggled.

"Why didn't he ever tell us? Why would he keep it a secret?" Carl said, not really expecting an answer.

The climb up the hill was so easy they couldn't believe it. They had hoped that their father would still be home, but he was already gone. It was only two, and he didn't have to leave until three, so why did he leave so early today? they wondered.

"Mom should be home soon," Carl said.

They were bursting with pride and wanted to share their feelings with their mother. Twenty minutes passed.

"Of all days, why did she have to be late today?" Mike lamented. The Ford was still parked on the gravel across the street, so the boys knew she hadn't driven somewhere. "Maybe she took a bus to pick up groceries or something.

The boys were getting worried. They had been home for over three hours, and their mother still wasn't home.

At six thirty, the phone rang. It was Dr. Stein. "Carl, I need to have you and Mike meet me right now in front of your house. Your father had a problem and has been transported to the hospital. Your mother is already there. Do you understand what I am telling you?" he asked. "We can talk more about the problem on the way to the hospital."

Carl did understand, but his knees were shaking so badly that he had to sit down. Mike was obviously anxious to hear what was going on. "Mike," Carl said, "Father is back in the hospital. Dr. Stein will take us there. We need to go out in front of the house right now."

Dr. Stein drove the boys directly to the naval hospital. On the way he explained that he had received an emergency call from a patient, and while at the hospital he learned of Bill's problem.

Dr. Stein filled the boys in the best he could about what he was able to find out. "Your father was speaking on the telephone to the emergency resident at the naval hospital, and in midsentence he collapsed. The doctor luckily heard the phone bang to the floor and immediately sent help."

Arriving at the hospital, Dr. Stein escorted the brothers directly into a waiting room where their mother was seated. It was obvious that she had been crying. When she saw her sons, she ran to them with arms open. She held them and thanked Dr. Stein and his family for bringing her boys to the hospital. Ruth asked the boys to sit down—she had something to tell them. The brothers slouched onto a sofa, but their anticipation of something being very wrong was overwhelming. "Your father is currently in the intensive care unit. The doctors are working with him, but we can't see him until the chief hospital surgeon gives us permission.

Bill was awake when they brought him in, but his speech was rather garbled."

Ruth explained, "The resident doctor sent a car to pick me up at the nursing home. At this point, I don't know what exactly happened to him. I am just so happy that you two are here. A few minutes ago, the nurse told me that we should have more information within the hour. I have asked several, but no one is willing to say much until the doctors finish performing their tests."

Dr. Stein put his hand on Ruth's shoulder and told her he and his family would stay around until she had definite word. She again thanked Dr. Stein and his family. Abe never left Carl and Mike.

It was another two hours before a doctor finally came into the waiting room. He walked to Ruth and sat down where all three family members could hear him.

"I have given Bill a complete examination. He had a slight stroke. I think that we got him here in time to prevent an even more serious problem. His right arm is numb, but not paralyzed. His speech is slurred, but that may very well go away—could be a day or a month, but I do not believe it is permanent," the doctor said.

"At this point, only time will tell. Bill was awake and alert when we brought him in. He told us that he got up from his nap about noon. He felt some pain in his neck and shoulder, but it was a different kind of pain than he has ever experienced before. He was alarmed enough that he called the hospital and that presence of mind probably saved his life. While he was on the phone describing his symptoms, he suddenly quit talking. Our resident doctor heard the noise of the phone when it hit the floor, and then the line went dead. He immediately dispatched an ambulance. Bill was unconscious when our technicians got to his home, but he regained consciousness during the ride to the hospital. He has been conscious ever since—a good sign," the doctor assured them.

"As I said, Bill was coherent enough to tell us everything that happened, and that helped us with our diagnosis. We got him here in time and have been giving him blood thinners to dissolve the clot. We will be keeping him for a few days, but I will let you and the boys see him for a few minutes. Bill was alert enough to know that his family would be worried, so as soon as he got to the hospital, he asked if someone could pick up his wife. It was lucky we caught her because she was just leaving when our driver spotted her. We all know the Spader family around here," the doctor said.

"We are working now to slow down his heart rate. He is still awake, but he will get groggy in a while. You can have five minutes, but don't start a lengthy conversation. I want him to rest and let our medicine do its job."

Dr. Stein assured the family that he would still be there when they got through with their visit.

Bill was awake and sitting up in bed when his family entered his room. He had tubes in both arms and was housed in an oxygen tent, but got a big smile on his face when he saw his family.

Ruth and her sons avoided talking about the visit to the library. They talked about their love for him and reassured him of how much they needed him to be part of their lives.

His voice was still slurred when he spoke. "We have a lot of things to do and talk about, so I will work hard to get well and try to be home in a few days. You boys take care of your mother, and don't let her fret about anything."

The doctor stood patiently by the door and then motioned for the three of them to leave. Ruth bent inside the tent and kissed Bill. The boys waved, but Bill could only wave with his left hand.

"There is nothing you can do here, so go home and take care of your boys," the doctor said.

Once outside the room, the doctor more fully described Bill's condition to Ruth, the boys, and Dr. Stein. Dr. Stein asked the doctor some specific questions, and after the doctor left, he gave a more simplified medical explanation that was very much appreciated by the family. He offered to drive the family home, and Ruth graciously accepted.

The family went to their living room and sat quietly for several minutes before anyone said anything. It was Carl who first spoke. "Why didn't Father want us to know about his military record? It is such a remarkable accomplishment. Why didn't he think that might be something we would have wanted to know?"

Ruth was sitting between her sons, and she took their hands in hers. "Your father is a quiet man. He doesn't want people congratulating him on an event that he has spent fifteen years trying to forget. He was forced to take the lives of many people that day, and regardless of how many lives he saved, he can't get those images out of his mind. Your father doesn't sleep well, and that is why I am always reminding you not to disturb when he is asleep. When we were first married, he used to talk in his sleep and often woke up screaming. His bad dreams had to do with him trying to save his men. He would sit up in bed and be soaking wet. I quietly reassured him that everything was fine, and as I wiped his forehead with a dampened cloth, I would tell him that I loved and cared about him. It was a difficult time for both of us. When they found that undiscovered piece of metal imbedded in his back, I thought that he might try to end his own life. That is when I would visit him so often and reassure him of my love. I would take him photos of you, Carl, as an incentive not to give up,"

"This isn't the first time that your father has had one of these attacks. It has happened several times before, but each time the episode passed without serious consequences. It isn't that your father has ignored the warning signs. It was just that he already knew what to look for—he knew that from talking to his doctors.

"Father's body is so banged up. When he talks about going into the hospital for some cosmetic surgery, it isn't to make his back look pretty. It's to remove scar tissue and sew together portions of broken muscle and tissue. His back has had to be rebuilt along with his buttocks and upper legs. You have never seen him in a swimming suit, and you probably never will. He has holes in his backside the size of your thumb. They all had to be sewn up and continually treated. Occasionally, little pieces of bone come to the surface of one of his scars. They protrude like slivers and have to be removed. It may have been a small piece of bone sliver that caused this stroke. We never know, we just pray.

"Your father is probably the most remarkable man I have ever known. He would work three jobs if I would let him, just to provide a better life for all of us. When one of you mention how you would like a new bike, or to go to Disneyland, or take a vacation, your father dies a little inside. He knows what you want and what you need. Oh, how he longs to be able to give you those things. He just can't. Your father would like to see you both enrolled in a private school similar to the one Abe will be attending, but again, it just isn't possible.

"Do you know that we have been putting ten dollars a month away toward your college education? It is a pittance of what you will need, but at least it is a way your father and I can feel like we are able to help. I don't want you two to feel like your desires are selfish. You are just normal, good kids who would like to have more than you have. Try to work hard in school and get an education so that you can someday help yourselves. It appears as though our possibilities of ever being wealthy are beyond our reach. We can only hope that you two can succeed where we have failed."

She hugged each of them. "There is a possible bright side, so you might as well know about that. Your father has had so many recurring hospital stays, the veterans examining board has been petitioned to review your father's disability case. We will know the results of that review within the month. If the board does like we have been told they might do, it is possible that your father will be entitled to a larger disability payment rather than the miniscule amount he gets now. He will still be allowed to work twenty hours a week if he desires, but he won't have to work at all if his health isn't up to it. That payment coupled with what I make at the nursing home might be enough for us to move to a nicer neighborhood, closer to a better school.

"What we have to do now is pray that he will pull through this latest attack. Everyone at the hospital is pulling for him. They don't say anything in front of me or you kids, but there is not a person in this hospital or this town that has anything to do with the military who doesn't know about the honors that have been bestowed upon your father. I don't believe that Dr. Stein or any of our neighbors know about the heroism of your father," Ruth said.

"Don't advertise about his valor. He's not unhappy that you found out. He would have told both of you someday, but he wouldn't want you to tell it to the neighbors or your classmates. It has a different meaning to him than it does to us," Ruth said.

Bill remained in the hospital for six more days and was then released.

Ruth and the boys took a bus to the hospital and brought Bill a change of clothing. After thanking the hospital staff, Bill and his family were taken home in the admiral's black limo. Neighbors looked out their windows as the long shiny vehicle stopped in front of the Spader home.

The navy ensign, who had driven Bill and his family home, assisted Bill into the house and helped him into a comfortable position in his favorite chair. Bill seemed to have made great strides during his latest hospital stay, and there was obvious movement in his right arm and hand. His speech was no longer slurred.

"Thank you for your help," Bill said to the young officer. The ensign saluted him as Ruth escorted him to the door.

Better Days

About an hour after the family arrived home, a knock came at the door. Carl opened the door and was surprised to see a tall man dressed in a dark-black suit. It was summer in San Diego, and the sight of the white-haired perspiring man was comical to Carl.

"Is this the residence of Captain William Morgan Spader, and is he at home?" the man asked.

Had Carl not gone to the library that day, he would have assumed that the navy officer had come to the wrong house.

"Yes, sir," Carl replied. "This is his residence, and he is at home."

"My name is Edgar Slaughton Prescott, and I am the chief liaison officer for the Veterans Administration, Department of Disability Services."

Carl snickered slightly when he heard the title and name, but Mr. Prescott either didn't hear him or chose to ignore the outburst. Carl's mother sure heard him though, and she gave Carl a tight-lipped chastising glare.

The man walked over to Bill and questioned, "You are Captain William Morgan Spader, United States Army?"

"I am," he said as he shook the man's hand. "Mr. Prescott, this is my wife Ruth, and our two sons, Carl and Mike."

The man politely nodded. "Captain Spader, I have been commissioned to deliver some documents to you that will require your approval and signature. I will explain fully the contents, and then if you wish to sign the papers, you may do so at this time."

If you desire to speak to your own lawyer, then we can postpone signing until after you have contacted council," Mr. Prescott said.

Bill jokingly asked the man if he was under arrest.

"Oh no, sir, forgive me. I didn't make my intentions understood," Mr. Prescott responded.

Ruth brought in a chair from the kitchen and offered it to the man. He accepted the chair and pulled it up next to the coffee table before sitting down. He placed a large white sealed envelope on the table and began to speak. "If our records are correct, you have been receiving a partial disability payment of $112 from the United States government for the past fifteen years. Is that correct?" he asked.

"I have. They come promptly on the first of every month," Bill answered.

"According to our records, you have already received $20,160. Is that correct?"

"Well, I haven't kept track to the penny, but I have to assume that your records are more accurate than my own," Bill said.

"In recent months, the Veterans Administration has been conducting a review of all disability cases that have occurred since December 7, 1941. In our discussions with the military doctors and staff at the San Diego Naval Hospital, it was their recommendation that your disability payments be modified."

Mr. Prescott then explained, "It is the unanimous decision of the Veterans Administration Disability Board, based upon other claims that have recently been brought to their attention, that your current disability payment will be retroactively modified."

Silence engulfed everyone in the room. Had the government discontinued Bill's pittance compensation? None of the family could believe it. Bill was about to say something when the man spoke again.

"The board of review, however, does not accept the recommendation of the 1944 Disability Review Board decision in your case. Based upon your past and continuing medical problems, they mutually agree that the 10 percent disability was insufficient."

Bill again was about to say something, but he waited to hear the man out.

"The current administration is concerned that veterans, such as you, were discriminated against. Each and every disability case since December 7, 1941, has been reviewed, and your case was one of those that they determined should be adjusted.

"It is the binding decision of the Veterans Administration that the status of your disability be reclassified. Our records indicate that you have had no less than thirty-seven major and minor surgical procedures over the past fifteen years. Our records also indicate that your health has been such that you have been extremely limited in opportunities for gainful employment, primarily because of your service related injury.

"If acceptable to you, the government of the United States of America is agreeable to reclassifying you as 90 percent disabled. As such, you will be entitled to a retroactive payment of $241,900 less the $20,160 you have already received. The Veterans Administration has also allowed for a loss of interest allowance of 5 percent. If acceptable to you, I am prepared to offer you a tax-free US government check in the amount of $232,848. Of course, the monthly disability payments you receive in the future will all be taxable," Mr. Prescott said.

Ruth put her hand over her mouth in disbelief. With the extra income, Bill would not have to work and could recuperate at home.

Thinking the meeting had ended; Bill arose and extended his hand to thank the VA representative. But Mr. Prescott didn't stand because he wasn't through talking. Bill slowly sat back down in his chair.

"If you desire to contact your own legal adviser, then you are free to do so. You have every right to challenge the findings of the board, and we will set a date for a formal hearing. If you desire to challenge the retroactive date, that is also your prerogative," Mr. Prescott advised.

The entire Spader family was speechless. Ruth was crying, and the boys were happily engaged in skipping around the room.

"I think I can accept that," Bill said with a sheepish grin on his face.

"Captain Spader, will you accept the terms of our proposal and accept this check, or would you rather have time to think it over and talk to your own attorney?"

Bill looked at Ruth and his two sons. "Well, advisors, what do you think? Should we accept the check?"

The entire Spader family burst into laughter. Ruth was in shock and went to the other overstuffed chair to sit down.

"It appears that we have a unanimous decision, and I waive any rights to legal representation. We gratefully accept the check. Please convey our deepest appreciation to your organization. We truly thank you from the bottom of our hearts," Bill said.

Bill signed the necessary paperwork and then cautiously accepted the check, almost in fear that the whole thing had been a horrible practical joke.

Mr. Prescott finally stood, making it evident to Bill that the meeting was over. He shook hands with Bill and nodded his head to each of the other family members. The entire family walked with him to the door and waved as he headed toward his car.

It was over, fifteen years of sacrifice and worry. They were no longer poor, and all of their material wants were within reach. Bill grasped Carl's shoulders and looked at him.

"I hate to be the one to tell you, but you are adopted. Your mother and I have kept it as a secret from you. Your great-grandparents were from England. One of them was Jack the Ripper, and the other one was Benedict Arnold. We just didn't have the courage to tell you until now."

Ruth and Mike broke into laughter. It took a few seconds before Carl realized that his father was actually joking.

It was over, and they watched through the window as the man climbed into his car to do next whatever a summer Santa does.

Carl raced into his bedroom and sat down at the desk. Boy did he have a story to tell, and his teacher was going to be amazed.